As High As the
Scooter Can Fly

As High As the
Scooter Can Fly

LIA NIRGAD

THE OVERLOOK PRESS
Woodstock & New York

First published in the United States in 2002 by
The Overlook Press, Peter Mayer Publishers, Inc.
Woodstock & New York

WOODSTOCK:
One Overlook Drive
Woodstock, NY 12498
www.overlookpress.com
[for individual orders, bulk and special sales, contact our Woodstock office]

NEW YORK:
141 Wooster Street
New York, NY 10012

∞ The paper used in this book meets the requirements for paper
permanence as described in the ANSI Z39.48-1992 standard.

Library of Congress Cataloging-in-Publication Data

Nirgad, Lia.
As high as the scooter can fly / Lia Nirgad.—1st ed.
p. cm.
1. Married women—Fiction. 2. Sisters—Fiction.
3. Flight—Fiction. I. Title.
PR9510.9.N57 A9 2002   823'.92—dc21   2002066314

Book design and typeformatting by Bernard Schleifer
Manufactured in the United States of America
FIRST EDITION
10 9 8 7 6 5 4 3 2 1
ISBN 1-58567-313-7

For my mother,
who showed me the beauty of words.

Contents

As High As the
Scooter Can Fly

ONCE UPON A TIME, but not so long ago, in a little house with a lovely garden, there lived a woman named Layla.

This woman Layla, of whom our story tells, was married to a man she did not love. He was not an evil man, but he was slow and quiet, and a cold, stagnant air wrapped him from dawn to dusk.

Layla also had three little daughters, fresh as strawberries, sweet as cream, filled with morning happiness.

This Layla, who now spent her time taking best care of her garden and her daughters, and even of the husband she didn't love, was once a young girl who cared for one thing only: she loved to travel, and whenever she had some time and some money, she'd pack a little bag and buy a little map, and travel along the dusty roads in search of an open space. But a strange thing had happened to her over the years, the strangest thing really, and she never ever left her house anymore, except for very little walks with her daughters.

Now Layla, I have said, loved an open space more than anything. And even if she took good care of her house and cleaned it very nicely, and filled the kitchen with wholesome food, and hung the laundry on the line very neatly, she didn't love the house, which was a strange little house, with twisted passages that always made her steps too small for comfort. Layla did love her garden, and she spent many hours there, pruning her roses and weeding her flower-beds, always with her back to the house.

And so Layla spent the years after her marriage locked up in her neat little house, though there never was a key, and there wasn't any lock. Layla hadn't very many visitors in this house of hers. People said it was cold, people said it was too far away. But every Saturday, Layla eagerly waited: she'd let her little girls pick oranges and lemons in the garden, and she'd make twelve bottles of lovely fresh juice and wait for her guests.

Her husband didn't really like guests to come to the house. He would sit among them, smiling politely, but still he was silent, and the air about him remained cold when they came and cold when they left and cold while they sipped their lovely juice. But Layla used to talk with her guests with words as quick as silver. She would wrap up her husband with her lovely quick words, so that the cold air about him didn't spread all over the room. She would talk while they came and talk while they left and talk while they sipped their lovely juice, and she would lift her little chin and hope with all her heart that they wouldn't notice the cold air that chilled her bones and made her fingers freeze.

Only when the guests would leave, only then did

Layla gather her words all back into her mouth, and she'd try to keep them all inside there, just to see if someone else would do the talking.

Now you mustn't think, because of this, that Layla was unhappy. She would weed her flower-beds and comb her daughters' hair, and she'd say to herself, How lucky I am to have my flowers and my girls, how lovely this is, how restful: my feet were so sore once, and my face so dusty, but now I can walk on soft carpets and nicely mowed grass, and never have blisters anymore.

But neither must you think, just because of this, that Layla was as happy as could be. She would fold the clothes and stack them up in little piles and find the best places for them in the closets, and she would say to herself, The spaces used to be bigger once, my legs used to be stronger, and there were so many places to see. But this husband of mine, with his cold hands and his tired arms, he loves his neat little spaces, and he doesn't even know how far the road lies.

But she never complained, our Layla, she knew she had promised to take care of the husband and do all the laundry, and promises must be kept. She also knew she had promised to love her husband, but love doesn't come by promise, and only true vows make for true love.

Layla also had three pretty sisters, who loved her very dearly.

The oldest sister was called Liora, and she lived in a

house very much like Layla's, but her plants were even nicer. In Liora's garden the roses were as big as orchids, and their colors changed with every sunset. Strange things were buried in Liora's garden, twisted cords which she kept after every childbirth: six children, all wrapped up six times in cord. Liora was a big, beautiful woman, and she took very best care, better than Layla even, of her husband and her lovely children. She would feed them all with spoons made of silver, and she knew how to make the most special dishes that kept them happy and strong. And if they were ever ill, she never called a doctor, she certainly didn't, she had just the right drops of golden fluid that would mend them in no time at all.

But there was a strange thing about Liora's food and medicine: they seemed to make her husband smaller and smaller, till he almost vanished and could hardly find his way in the big house she filled. And her children, those six lovely, strong children, why did they always remain so small, their fingers never bigger than their mother's little toe?

Now it may seem strange to you, but no one seemed to mind all of this, they were all so happy, they never wanted to be any bigger. That's the way happiness can be sometimes, as you might very well know.

The second sister was called Lenore, and was just a year or so older than Layla. Lenore was the truly beautiful one, her hair as smooth as water, her eyes the color of tender violets, her heart so cold you'd be afraid to touch it.

This sister never married, and she certainly had no children. She lived in a tiny flat in town, all glass and perfectly whitewashed walls. She was always neatly dressed, her fingers so pretty and her nails so long, she could stab a hole in any man's heart and dig it right out. And when she did, then her heart became even colder, so cold that it froze, and her eyes, those eyes of tender violet, they became a cyanide blue.

The youngest sister was called Lihi. This sister was pretty too, like all the others, but her hair was often greasy. She never lived very long in any one place, but all the places she lived in looked alike, with cracks in the walls and dust all over. Lihi hadn't taken care of any man yet, and she hadn't learned any tricks yet, so she had to be very careful, as her older sisters kept reminding her. She was so careful she didn't even have to be afraid, which made her feel very happy inside and made all her sisters very proud of her. And if something came up, a wrinkle on that smooth way she glided through her days, she had a lovely bracelet, a bracelet of seven charms, that could do away with any little disturbance.

Layla had yet a younger sister, the truly youngest one, but she had been dead these many years. Luna was her name, Luna the star-child, whose eyes were as deep as a sigh, Luna, who had heard every cold and Loveless Wind and sat in her highchair moaning while the Winds hurt her inside. Sweet, sad, little Luna, whose dolls would break with every northern gale, brave little Luna, who had tried so hard, so long, till that cruel day when a great Typhoon tore her apart.

All these sisters loved each other very dearly. Even Lenore, the one with the cold heart and the changeful eyes, cared for her sisters more than anything else in the world. They loved each other so, that even little Luna, she who had been taken by the Loveless Winds, could come and visit. But there was a promise they all had to keep, or else the Winds would possess her forever. A certain rule had to be followed, a little, petty rule, a seemingly easy rule, of which you are yet to hear.

And so they would all meet and drink their coffee and tell of their sorrows, but only of those worth telling. None spoke of Lenore's chilly heart, and no one asked why Liora's children never grew—though they did mention the shriveling husband, with a forgiving smile. Lihi never said how afraid she was at nights, and Layla—always the most silent among her sisters—she only talked about her three lovely girls.

Now you mustn't think Layla's sisters never noticed that strange air which wrapped up her husband like a shroud. And you mustn't think that they never whispered, after she had left, how dull her hair had become. But Layla had many a smile, a full bag of them. She had this wonderful, special smile that looked happy to the very tip of the nose, and she'd tell them how happy she was, and sit in her chair with her legs neatly crossed like a very grown woman, offering to teach them her special smile—what could they do but envy her?

Now Layla was no liar. And if she said she was happy, well there she was, with that lovely garden and her cozy ways, and that soothing morning quiet of familiar days. And the husband, well, he wasn't evil, not at all. And when she sat among her sisters, with all their little tricks and secret fears, she almost liked him, sometimes.

Indeed, by now Layla's heart had shrunk into a very little lump, and when her stomach was full enough, or even better, when her belly was filled with babies, she hardly felt she had any heart at all. And when she'd talk to Luna she'd say: "You needn't ever worry about me, I'm all snug and safe now, and the dusty roads lie far behind me."

It was only on Tuesday afternoons, when the girls went to visit their aunt Liora, that she would walk the house with a restless foot, her shoulders shrunk, her arms afraid to move in the twisted passages of her small, chilly home. It was then that she'd gaze in the mirror, wondering what had become of her face, once so curious, so happy. It was then that she'd hear the song of the Loveless Winds, a weary song of wisdom and oblivion, and she'd close the windows and draw the curtains, hoping to shut out the sound.

It is on one of these Tuesdays, a damp and heartless Tuesday on the seventh year of Layla's marriage, that our story begins.

1
scalded thighs and
icecreamdrop smiles

THE HOUSE WAS EMPTY, as always on a Tuesday, but our Layla was never lazy, and even now she walked about quickly, and her movements were neat: she always remembered her mother's advice, and never walked from one room to another with empty hands. So she picked up the dirty socks in the bedroom she shared with her husband and used her spare hand to smooth the sheets, and she went to the bathroom to take the rest of the wash, and then walked back to the bedroom with the clean clothes she had found on the wet floor. She was only trying to get from her room to the washer, but on her way she kept finding so many things out of place, so many shoes and books, so many toys and socks, that she walked back and forth with those quick steps, her hands always fuller, dirty clothes stuffed under her arms, an old newspaper under her chin, till the toys started falling from her hands, which

were all dry and nervous, itching to cry. But she was never
lazy, our Layla, and she knew just how much comfort
there was in a clean surface. So she kept walking back and
forth, like a dancing, breathless bee, until, suddenly, it was
all done.

But when she tried to make some tea, just to sit there
and watch her lovely surfaces, her nervous, itchy hands
spilled the steaming water all over her thighs, and she
started to cry.

Now there was another thing Layla had learned from
her mother: Never stop what you're doing just because of
pain. So even now, with tears on her face, she made the tea
and walked out to the garden, where she sat with her back to
the street, trying to see only that patch of green where the
house cast no shadow, her very own spot in this whole place
she tended, right between the rosebush and the pine tree.

This pine tree was a very big tree, so big it made the
house look quite tiny, and its roots grew wide apart. A
whole big chunk of Layla's garden lay in the shadow of
this tree, whose dry needles covered the ground and
smothered the plants growing about it. It was one of
Layla's little self-inflicted tasks to rake up these needles
and clear the plants, which could hardly grow under all
this dry stuff.

Under the shadow of the pine tree there stood, ever
since Layla first came to the house, an old little scooter.
Her husband had wanted to throw it out, but she would-
n't, and he didn't really mind, though he liked to mention
it from time to time, just to tease her. Even her sisters had
said it was old and rusty and didn't fit in, but Layla, she

thought: "What a sweet little scooter it is." She let it stand there, all covered with dry leaves, and she'd say to them: "Some day I'll put flowerpots on it, and it will be absolutely beautiful." And whenever she felt happy, she'd let her girls stand on the scooter and pretend they were traveling to Neverland.

But on this damp and heartless Tuesday, when she started clearing the pine needles, with her thighs aching so badly, she removed them from the scooter too. And then she looked around to see there was no one there, and got on the scooter, and said: "Oh I wish you could fly."

And because seven long years had passed, and the time was right, it did.

Yes, dearest. Just like that.

Now you mustn't imagine, just because this scooter could fly, that it flew very quickly or very high. Please remember, it was an old little scooter, and even magic gets rusty after a while. But this only made Layla happier. After all, she wasn't used to flying and had hardly left her house for seven long years. So she flew quite carefully, hoping no one would notice. It was a quiet neighborhood, you see, the kind people leave in the mornings and return to just before dusk. So she didn't really have to worry. She had a whole delicious hour to practice this careful flying around her garden. It was such a gentle little scooter, she even tried it inside the house, and it took the corners very carefully. She was really having a lot of fun, which isn't a very seriously enchanted thing to do, but that's what she did anyway. And by the time the girls came back she had already carried her new flying scooter back to the pine tree and carefully covered it with pine needles in a seemingly careless way. And she promised herself not to tell anyone about it, not even her sisters.

All this was not necessarily pleasant, of course. It is one thing to stay home and fold up your laundry when you're a grown woman who has decided to stop tramping about, and quite another thing to keep on doing it when you have a magic scooter all to yourself. You know, don't you, how tempting a flying scooter can be. You'd want to go all the way to Limpopo, wouldn't you? Or Mozambique. Who could stop you from going all the way to China just before dinner? And Layla, she wanted to go to Alaska and Prague. She wanted to see Malaysia and Australia and Istanbul too, all those long-sounding, soft-sounding places.

A quandary, that's what it became.

She was actually losing sleep over it.

And so, even though Layla was careful, and no one knew what she had hidden under her pine tree, some little things started to change. These changes were so small, even she hardly noticed at first. There was less and less food in the house, but that wasn't very easy to discover because she had so many things in her freezer, and so many more things in her pantry, that her husband never knew when she skipped shopping. She didn't stop picking up the toys, she just put them on the shelves in the girls' room, forgetting which toy belonged in which basket. But there were so many toys, and so many baskets, her daughters never noticed what they were playing with.

And she stopped changing the sheets every week, but no one had ever cared about that anyway. Only Layla could feel that horrible damp softness of a sheet that needs changing after seven sad, lonely nights.

No one seems to notice, she thought after a few weeks, seven perhaps; no one ever notices; no one needs to know; I could fly about from time to time, and no one would know. Surely there can be no harm in it. It will be my very own secret. Indeed, she was very good about keeping secrets, our Layla; it was one of the things she was best at. It gave her this special smile, which the girls called Mommy's icecreamdrop smile.

But her sisters, they knew her well. They never spoke of icecreamdrop smiles. They said, "Layla looks like she's swallowed a fucking canary." And when they asked her she just smiled that same secret smile, in a very slow, almost teasing way, and said, "Oh, nothing." But they knew she was lying.

Her sister Liora gave her some golden medicine, just in case there was something wrong. But our Layla, she was a prudent one, and she never took any of the stuff, which could make you so small you'd never find your way out of bed anymore. ("She's found a lover," Lenore said to Liora, but Liora, she didn't like that kind of talk. She said,

"Maybe she's found something else, she's a grown woman, you know.")

And in time even the husband, even he, whose eyes were so slow, had come to see. And he said to himself, This wife of mine, her feet are getting restless. But he didn't say a word to her, you see, he was so afraid she'd ask him to come along.

It is now time to learn a few things about this husband. You already know that he wasn't evil, and you know how quiet he was. He was so quiet he could hear his own bowels every time they moved. This quiet husband had met Layla when she was still dusty with traveling, and he had thought, This woman, her feet are so light and her eyes so bright, maybe she can take me with her. But his hands moved so slowly, his eyes were so heavy, and the air about him so cold, that the very opposite thing had happened, and it was Layla who changed her ways, she who had promised so much and vowed so little. And he, he forgot that distant moment when he first had seen her, forgot his wish to travel the roads. It had all happened so long ago, and had lasted for such a short little while.

And so, as the years passed, his limbs froze, and only his tongue sometimes shivered inside his mouth, longing for something sweet.

By the time our story begins, the husband's dearest wish was to sleep whenever he could, and if he ever spoke of other countries, it was only to have his neat stack of clothes all folded up in the very same way but somewhere else, some place with a lake nearby. And he never left the house anymore, except to go to work, of course.

But he wouldn't mind if Layla did, you see. He did remember her lovely, dusty, end-of-the-world smile.

And Layla, she was smart. She never once mentioned the scooter. She only started saying things like, "I'd like to go to town today," or, "I'm meeting Lenore for lunch."

To break ground, as it were.

And he was happy, you see, because he didn't want a restless woman on his hands. And also because he still loved that brightness in her eye. He was just a sad little husband, remember, not an evil one. "You can go wherever you like," he'd say, and he'd lay in the dark and hope she wouldn't go too far away.

That's where the trouble began.

There was Layla, with her scooter, and all the permission she needed. She felt proud, our Layla. She thought, There's no stopping me, no one will stand in my way now. For seven long years I have been patient—now I'm back again, as reckless as ever.

And the joy of it went way beyond the tip of her nose, which remained very discreetly calm.

2
a whole week forward,
a whole week back

It was then, just then, that Layla went on her first real trip. She didn't just go anywhere; she thought about it first. She needed an open space, as open as could be. She considered the desert, so close to her house, open all the way round, but she didn't really like the heat, which always made her smiles crackle with dust. So she got on her scooter and said, "Alaska." Because it's so empty; because it's so cold; because the sound of it is so icily brisk.

Now the scooter, I have said, was a gentle one. It flew quite slowly, and never very high, which was fine with Layla, afraid as she was of heights. And would you believe it? There was such a big icecreamdrop smile on her face, and such a big end-of-the-world smile right beneath it, she became quite invisible.

All night long she flew. It was quite a long time really, and she was starting to feel cold. And tired. She almost felt whiny. I've become like my husband, she thought, I've lost the magic of the road. But she wouldn't give up, not now that she had the scooter and was just about to make it all the way to Alaska, which was really far away, much farther than she had ever traveled before.

By the time she got to Alaska she was so tired, she just wanted to sleep. All tucked up in snow, our Layla, it was getting quite uncomfortable really; and by the time she fell asleep she missed her bed, and she missed her girls, she even missed her little house.

But she didn't miss her husband.

The light was gray when she woke up from her little nap, all stiff and cold. Little tears, unnoticed, had frozen on her eyelashes; little tears shed who knows when, perhaps in her sleep, as happened so often to our smiling Layla.

I wish there were someone here to show me the way, she thought, almost miserably.

And because she was being watched, watched anxiously, by those who had watched her since the day she was born, a little mink, sitting all very comfortable by an oak tree, answered. "There's nothing to see, really," said the mink. "It's white all over."

"That isn't a very encouraging thing to say," said Layla, her mouth as cross as a raisin.

"You mustn't be cross," the mink answered, in a cold little voice.

"Well, you're not one to stop me," she replied, and her face was getting quite warm by now. "I'm always as cross as I please. Who are you, anyway?"

"Don't be so rude," he calmly answered. "I'm here to show you Alaska. Isn't that what you asked for?"

"You just said there was nothing to see," said Layla, who was very good at spotting a contradiction, no matter how wide apart the terms.

"There isn't. That's what I'm trying to show you," said the mink. "You see, it's white all over. And if you walk a whole week forwards, or if you walk a whole week back, it will still remain quite white all over." The mink now cuddled up in a little hole in the tree-trunk and pretended to fall asleep.

"You can't go to sleep now, it isn't fair," Layla cried. And would you believe it, she stamped her foot.

The mink seemed quite impressed. "Oh dear, a foot stamper, a regular Highness, an actual Princess, aren't you. I hadn't realized. I truly ask for forgiveness." And he sat up very gravely.

"Yes I am," said Layla, very glad there was no one around who knew her. "I'm princess Layla, and I haven't just walked all the way here, you know. I've come on my flying scooter."

"Oh goodness, a flying scooter it is," said the mink.

"So there, now you must show me the way, mustn't you," said Layla, and she stamped her other foot, just because the mink seemed to take stamping so very seriously.

"Oh dear, but you see, it's still white all over, princess or no princess," replied the mink, with a nasty little smile.

"So I can still cuddle up in my hole and get some rest, can't I."

"I'll find out for myself," said Layla, her nose all tingly with tears. "But now I have to hurry back home. It must be morning already."

So she got on her scooter and flew all the long way back, and when she got home she just parked her little scooter under the pine tree, shook all the snow off her hair, and walked into the house using her front door key, with an ask-me-no-questions face.

And her husband, he didn't ask any questions, that's the wrong of it: surely she would have told him, right then.

Because you see, although she kept her little chin up all day long, and although she kept it up even in her sleep, she was madly disappointed with her trip.

But did she ever say even a word of this disappointment, even to herself?

Did she have herself a good cry?

Indeed she didn't. Not our Layla. It was so cold there, she furiously told herself, and that scooter is so small, there's hardly any room on it; I really don't have to do this, I'm a grown woman, aren't I?

And yet, she was so disappointed, she would have cried very snugly in someone's arms. But those arms, remember, were such tired arms; and Layla's tears, they were always so heavy.

3

so eager,
so starved

And so our Layla, she started to fret. Back in that little house with the twisted little corridors, she was now doing more laundry than ever. It was raining day and night, but still she washed and washed, and there were clothes drying all over the house, on sofas and chairs, along the bookshelves, covering every little space, every edge.

It's such a tiny scooter, she'd she'd say to herself as she looked in the mirror. It makes me look quite ridiculous.

So I have a scooter, she'd mutter, but I also have this lovely house, and so many things to do in it.

And this also: Let's face it, I always ended up alone and crying on those trips of mine, didn't I?

All of which was true in a way, but in one way only.

I was never really all that brave, she kept telling herself, while folding the laundry ever so neatly.

It's not so hard to be braver than that husband of mine,

she said to herself, moving around the house, quicker and quicker, bumping into the furniture till her legs were all black and blue.

I'm perfectly happy just as I am, she said to herself, and her hair was so bitter and dry you could burn it all up with a spark of pity.

Now if you are still wondering what it is that the mink actually did to her, if you are saying, Well he only told her there was nothing to see, and perhaps there really wasn't, then you have never walked a twisted corridor in your life. Because if you had, if you had ever felt that tightening of your step, if you had ever brushed your shoulder against the wall twenty times a day just walking from one room to another in your own house, then you would know how eager Layla had been, how starved, when she first came to Alaska. And if you had ever felt your hair clinging greasily to your forehead on a simple summer evening, your armpits trickling with sweat, your shoulders tense, your thighs flabby, you would know her sense of defeat.

But she never said a word of it, of course she didn't, not even to herself.

So now our Layla, our very own Layla, she who would spring up with a smile at any time, now she hardly got out of bed in the mornings, and she'd hobble to the bathroom, trying to keep her mind off her new, secret sorrow. That silly, childish sorrow. Sorrow for reasons unheard of, as far as she was concerned—and therefore to be ignored.

Not to be fussed about, that's for sure.

Definitely not to be talked about—surely there wasn't anything to say?

So she kept up the cleaning, and the washing, and of course she gave those little girls their food and brushed out their hair in the mornings, as gently as ever, or almost so. She was so clever with her hands, our Layla, she could hold one girl on her arm and help the others with their coats and talk on the phone all at once, and even then she was thinking of something completely different. But she didn't read them so many stories now, and she hardly ever baked their favorite biscuits, and she never, ever talked to them of fairies anymore.

Day after day passed, and the shadows under her eyes, they became so blue, the girls were almost scared. But they were so small, those girls, and the trouble, it became so big, how could they put their little fingers on it? Only at nights did the younger one cry in her sleep, dreaming of hunger. Layla was so upset, she could almost slap the child every time she looked into her round, worried eyes.

Oh she was angry, our Layla, she was so angry she could slap anyone—her husband, her daughters, that horrible little mink. But more than anything, or anyone, she could slap herself black and blue.

For having stopped so quickly.

For having scared so easily.

For letting go so fast.

But now her sisters, those lovely live sisters and the lovely dead one too, they decided it was time to do something about Layla. They didn't hear her muttering, and they didn't see the bruises on her legs, all covered up with long, awkward clothes. But they did notice that new stillness in her voice—that smiling voice of hers, which had always been so glib with gladness—and they did notice that new dryness of her hair. But most of all they noticed how quiet she had become on the phone, and that new way she had of saying, "Nothing, nothing really," whenever they asked what was going on.

And so they all met, this time in Lenore's apartment, and they sat there with their legs crossed and their hair neatly fixed, as they always did when Lenore was around, and they said, "This must be figured out." Because they really cared about Layla, you see, and they were very, very sure, that keeping a secret from them couldn't be good for her.

Not at all.

Not one bit.

"I'll visit her on Sunday," said Liora, the eldest. "I'll bring her some of my sweet-and-sour soup, and I'm sure she'll tell me in no time at all."

"And I'll visit her on Monday," said Lenore, the second. "I'll bring her my special double-action purifying mask, and I'm sure she'll tell me as soon as I walk through the door."

"And I'll go on Tuesday, and I'll bring some pizza and Coke," said Lihi, the youngest. "Maybe she'll tell me."

"But I'll go every night, and I'll smell her dreams," said Luna, the dead, Luna the tender, whose heart still ached every time she sensed any pain.

And so they all finished their coffee and said their good-byes.

All except Luna, who never drank anymore.

And so, on Sunday, just as she had promised, Liora came to her sister's house. She wore big white clothes with no buttons in them, and she carefully carried a dish of her sweet-and-sour soup. She made Layla sit at the table (remember she was the eldest), and she served her the soup, as sweet as birthdays, as sour as all the tears you've ever cried. It was a difficult soup to swallow, and Liora had made it especially sour this time. Layla ate it, one spoonful birthday sweet, two spoonfuls old tears, and her eyes were so dark you couldn't see where she was looking.

"You're too pale and thin," said Liora, with unblinking eyes. "The floor is dirty and there's dust on the shelves. And look what you've done to your laundry. All the colors have run."

By now Layla had finished her soup and her face was as confused as could be, her eyes quite sweet, her mouth quite sour. She knew very well that her oldest sister could find every black-and-blue spot on her body, so she said, "Well, you see, I have this scooter. It flies. I'm not very good at it yet, but I'm practicing.

"I keep bumping into things," said Layla, "it's very tiring, really," and she just managed a little, sad icecream-drop smile.

"Oh," said Liora, "now I see." And she gave Layla

some good travel advice and went home all very pleased with herself.

On Monday, just as she had promised, Lenore came to her sister's house. She wore shiny pants and a satin black shirt with brass zippers across the shoulders, and she brought the double-action purifying mask she always kept in her bathroom, her wondrous bathroom, a bathroom you could walk into and never leave for a week, full of creams and perfumes and lotions which could do away with any trace of sorrow or longing.

She now made Layla wash her face with ice-cold water and then carefully put the mask on. It was a bi-colored mask, blue to wipe off the fear, black to clean out the rage. Layla lay back on the sofa, her nose and forehead covered with blue, her cheekbones and chin in black, her mouth and ears meticulously clean to better hear and speak. Lenore sat just behind her, waiting for the mask to crack dry.

"You've stopped shaving your armpits," said Lenore, her violet eyes quite narrow. "And look at your eyebrows, they've become quite bushy again."

By now the mask was dry and Layla went to wash it off, all the fear now hidden in her ears, all the rage in her mouth. She knew very well that her sister would notice in no time at all, so she said, "You see, I've got this scooter, I've been taking all kinds of trips with it, to all kinds of places.

"There's places where I can't even find a mirror," said Layla, "so you see, eyebrows and shaving aren't so simple anymore," and she put on quite a nice end-of-the-world smile.

"Oh," said Lenore, "I see." And she gave Layla her own little make-up kit, and went home all very pleased with herself.

On Tuesday, just as she had promised, Lihi came to hers sister's house. She wore a pair of jeans and a very old sweater, which had belonged to their father. And she brought with her a huge pizza and a large Diet Coke. She sat next to her older sister and ate most of the food, gulping the Coke quite loudly. "Lenore and Liora say you have a scooter," said Lihi. "They say it flies. They say it can go quite far."

"Oh yes it does," said Layla, and she did a great big tip-of-the-nose smile. "I've flown all the way to Alaska."

"Oh," said Lihi, "That's wonderful." And before she went home, all quite excited really, she gave her sister her very own bracelet, the bracelet of seven charms.

And every night, just as she had promised, Luna came to her sister's house, wearing nothing but Wind. And she smelled her sister's dreams, those sad, endless dreams in which Layla would go from one party to another, feeling as lonely as a sigh. "I have a flying scooter," Layla moaned in her dream, "but there's nowhere to go, it's so cold and empty all over."

Tenderly, patiently, loving little Luna sniffed dream after bitter dream. It could almost make her cry, that stale smell of sorrow, the acrid stench of despair. "He was mocking me," Layla cried in her dream, silent as a ghost. "He let me say I was a princess: I was so proud for one little moment, and then it didn't even matter."

Now Luna, she could have mended Layla's dreams in no time at all. That was definitely something she could do. And indeed, she had often done just that, floating into her sisters' nightmares on a summer breeze, giving them a dreamland kiss of undivided love. But she wouldn't do it this time: Layla's dream had such a smell of serious business—she just sat there, holding her sister's sleepy hand, waiting for a whiff of rainbow. She knew her sister's dreams, how they'd smooth out just before dawn, letting her wake with fresh, clear eyes. But this dream was different; it remained crumpled till the very end. "I see," she sadly said to herself, and vanished just before the husband awoke from his heavy sleep.

Forgot all about him, haven't you? So much trouble, who'd think he'd still be there, right there in Layla's bed? But of course he was there, breathing as smoothly as ever, while Layla lay next to him, so close to the edge it was a wonder she never fell off. It was the seventh year, remember, the year of sleeping painfully, afraid of falling, afraid of touching, afraid of ever waking up again.

Did he really feel nothing, you ask again, and your eyes are so big with wonder. Nothing, I tell you, and someday, perhaps, you shall hear how it came to happen that his heart turned so deaf with fear, even screams couldn't touch it. But that's another story, and we must now come to the evening when Layla first told him about the scooter.

It was seven days after Lihi's visit, seven weeks since Layla's trip to Alaska. I'm not doing this ever again, she thought; so I might as well tell him all about it. And she told him, smiling her little oh-it-means-nothing kind of smile, a smile she did with her eyes mostly, looking down at the words coming out of her mouth. "It flies," she told him, "but it's really slow and can't even go as high as our rooftop."

"Oh, so that's all it can do," he said, and he tried to do Layla's little smile, but his heart ached with fear.

"You'll be careful, won't you," he said in his softest voice, and Layla was so ashamed she almost wept. He really believes me, she thought, maybe I should ask him to come along.

But she knew she wouldn't, you see. That's why she felt so ashamed.

Because even though she was such a dutiful wife, and even though she felt sure she'd never ride that scooter again, she couldn't really tell him how far, how alone, she had wanted to go. Next thing you know, she'd have to tell him how little she loved him, and that was something she never, ever did. She would say, "Your arms are so tired," or she'd say, "That silent air about you makes me freeze." But she never said, "I do not love you." She'd only cry in bed, sometimes, when she first was married, and then she'd say to him, "It's just that I don't know very much about love. Teach me."

She really thought he could, you see. She'd say to herself, "This husband of mine, he says he loves me, and no matter how often I cry in the mornings, no matter how much my hair frizzles with rage, no matter how heavy his arms and how lonely my dreams, he still insists that he does. So he must know something about this thing called Love, which I haven't yet learned."

Now you mustn't think, just because of this, that Layla really knew nothing of love. Of course she did. She had loved hard and quick, she had loved almost recklessly, till the Winds screamed in her ears; she had loved so sharp, so drunk, so muddy, she never wanted to do it again.

So you see, when the husband first came to her and said that he loved her, in that quiet voice of his, she thought, How nice it could be to do his kind of love, how peaceful. Maybe this is a good kind of love, a kind that doesn't rip you up inside. A kind of love you wouldn't suffer for. And she told him, as truthful as ever, "I've loved a man so hard I almost died. I'll never love you that way. But if you'll make me food when I'm hungry, and if you'll give me a drink when I'm thirsty, I'll find some pleasant love to give you."

And he agreed, you see, he wanted her so. That's the pain of it.

And she knew just how little "pleasant" means. That was the sin of it.

Because in a way, no matter how partial or painful a way, she did know how overwhelming love could be.

So that even when she said to herself, "How restful this is," and even when she said to herself, "Well, at least it's made to last," the coldness spreading inside her for seven long years nearly killed her. But only Luna, Luna the tender, Luna of the soft, bottomless eyes, knew this about Layla. Only she knew how painful that cold could be, worse than the worst kind of love. The other sisters—the mild, the daring, and the young—they couldn't know, they had never done that worst kind of love, and it seemed to them nothing could be worse. And Layla, she didn't tell them, no she didn't; she just did her grown-up smiles.

And so, on that evening when Layla told her husband about the scooter, and when they agreed that it wasn't a very dangerous—or even exciting—kind of scooter, they both knew they were lying. Because it wasn't hard to guess how far she could go, if only she found a little courage somewhere in her treasure-chest.

But still, there she was, lying next to him, one secret shared, two to go. And it felt quite nice, she thought, lying just like that with the girls still sleeping and the scooter outside, in its proper place, duly accounted for.

There's nothing to be ashamed of, she thought. I'm a dutiful wife and a mother of three, and this mink, even this scooter, well, they can't take it away from me, can they? They can't make me give it all up.

And when she looked in the mirror next morning she saw a big, tip-of-the-nose smile, right there were it was supposed to be, right there where it always had been, except for that short, crazed escape of hers, years and years ago, when tears had been so plentiful. And when she looked at herself right in the eye, oh so serenely, with that no-fuss-no-nonsense look she had learned along with many other useful lessons of childhood, she felt so clever, so happy, she started doing her smiles all day long, even when no one was watching.

You see, she thought she had learned her last lesson ever.

She thought she had finally settled down.

4
a tale of
awesome sadness

So now came some early spring cleaning, now her phone talks with Liora were full of recipes, and her meals full of spice. But she didn't talk very often with her other sisters, who always asked about the scooter. "It's okay," she'd say, "but I'm quite fed up with it really."

The little house was shinier than ever now, and the husband, oh, he was hugged all over the place. Layla was clinging to him so hard she almost baffled him to death. And the girls, those lovely three girls—what a fuss of clothes and hairpins, what a cascade of stories and games —Mommy's more fun than ever, they thought.

But they never saw that icecreamdrop smile of hidden gladness anymore.

As for the Winds, they were humming about, quite content really. They weren't gushing as of yet; they weren't storming, not at all. Just a steady, swirling gale, something you'd notice only after a while, after you'd picked up the fifth sheet of paper, after you'd smoothed out your hair for the fifth time. The laundry was gently dancing on the line, the thinnest pine branches swaying ever so slightly. But anyone with any sense at all could tell: the Loveless Winds had had their say.

And they were definitely, absolutely, pleased with themselves.

And now, dearest, you must finally learn more about the Loveless Winds. Listen carefully, only see that there aren't any children around. Let's not frighten the children with a tale of such awesome sadness.

No one knows how the Winds came to be, no one knows their whys and their whos, few even know their name. And yet, dearest, you yourself have surely heard them blow on some shriveled dawn, surely you've felt them creaking in your bones, twirling about in a taunting question mark, perhaps you've even seen them at work on some cruel day. Think well, try to remember, wasn't there a Wind blowing on that day you'd like to forget?

Beware of the Winds, dearest, for they are crafty, and their voice is smooth, they've met the like of you time and again—wide-eyed, somewhat worried, just a trifle scared —and they know just what it is that you want to hear.

Oh how far you'll go, dearest, once you enter the realm of the Loveless Winds! No one who saw you lying in your cradle, no one who saw your eager grasp on the day you were born, would ever think you'd go so far. Far, far away, to a boggy land of gloom and despair, with the

Winds always there, humming in your ear, promising to guide you on those slippery paths. Will they really show you the way? Of course they will. They'll take you to valleys of fear, they'll lead you on to swamps of pain, and sure enough, soon you'll be begging them to lead you to safer pastures. And if the light is always dim there, and if the greens be always gray, you'll settle dearest, you'll be only too glad to settle after a toss and fling with the Loveless.

Has no one ever returned? Has no one come back from that land of mild horror and fierce disillusion? Hasn't anyone drawn up the map that will show you the paths of the simple and the brave, the path of the lucky, all those paths that could steer you away from the Land of the Loveless?

Yes, dearest, some have returned. Some have come back and told their tattered snatch of a story.

So listen, dearest, listen well: perhaps indeed you shall find the path of the wise.

It all began on a shrill and gray November day, when a future mother of five was herself a hopeful youth. It was her wedding day, and there were flowers all about her, flowers in her ready hand and flowers in her raven hair, when she happened to look in the mirror. Of course she looked, how could she help it, she was a bride after all. Only this bride looked just a trifle too long, just a bit too sharply, and with more than a slight flicker of doubt and worry.

Now mirrors, you should know, are sly, slippery things; a Loveless Wind could hide in any one of them. Indeed, those Winds love a polished mirror above all, it is there that they lurk for the weak of heart, who come gazing in search of an answer. How quickly the Wind will pounce at their reflection, how firmly it will cling, how steadily it will gaze back at them, wishing to see itself just for once! As for those bewildered souls, even as they look themselves in the eye, it is the Loveless' shimmer they will find; and a haunting tune that will warn them never to give up their questioning, never to be seduced by love, never duped by devotion, never, ever to give away their heart.

And so, as that future mother of five looked in the fateful mirror, a cold Wind started singing its flutey tune. Such quiet wisdom she seemed to hear in that voice, such ageless wisdom of moderation and well-beaten paths. Oh how that Wind beguiled her! It was such a slip of a tune at first, and yet, quickly enough, she was listening closely, eagerly, lending that Wind much more than an ear, lending it her very own words to sing with. Was she worried, asked the Wind. Of course she was, it smoothly replied, but of course. So many things could indeed go wrong, so many things could fall short of expectation. There was such a vast margin of error in her choice, of course. And yet . . . and yet . . . Quick and slithery the words danced about her, quick and slithery, telling her how little need there was for real worry, singing of the folly of love and infatuation, gently, oh so gently mocking every fond dream she still cherished, telling her how easy it was to shrug it all off.

Just that flicker of doubt in her eye?
Just that shade of worry on her cheek?

Is that all it took?

How unfair it seems, why, haven't you also sat by a mirror, perhaps on the very day of your wedding? Haven't you had your flicker and shade? Aren't we all entitled to just a bit of doubt? Of course we are. Entitled. Oh yes. Condemned, if you like. The Winds wouldn't ever argue that point. You may have all the doubts you like; they, for their part, will sing their tune. And if it's fairness you seek, dearest, why, you can always refrain from listening.

Only it's such a tempting song at first: those nagging, taunting words you've heard so often in your heart, how beautiful they become when the Winds lend them their tune, how true they ring, how powerful! Think for yourself: what would you do if the Winds came to you? Wouldn't you listen? Is your heart so calm, is your love so easy, that no Wind could ever tempt you at all? Oh dearest, if your answer is yes, you are indeed one of the fortunate. And if you have ever listened, and then chased them off with a brave smile, even then you could count yourself among the lucky. For most of us, dearest, hear the tune of the Loveless with every breath we take.

So as she sat there, and as she heard that sober tune so many a bride has heard before her, she found herself shrugging just the slightest of careless shrugs. By then, of course, a Loveless Wind had swiftly clad her cold reflection. And when she looked into those green eyes, she could almost hear them whisper, "It will do."

"It will do," she whispered once more. Just in case.

And she felt actually grateful when she saw the shade of worry lift from her cheek.

And the flicker of doubt? All gone. Of course it was, off and away along with all that childish stuff and nonsense. All it took was the swiftest of shrugs, followed by that quick, earnest whisper.

And if there was a new, raised eyebrow suddenly arching above her steady eye, what of it? She saw it, of course she did. She was still looking in the mirror, wasn't she, but surely it was no price at all for the calm hue of her cheek: There she was, already, just in time for the first solemn chords that came wafting in, chasing away any trace of that other song.

Here came the bride, taking it all in her stride.

Oooh, how the Winds sighed with pleasure. She'll be ours now, they hummed, she'll come looking for us again, right here in the mirror, and we shall see ourselves every day now, she'll give us her lovely green eyes to see with, and they'll be lovelier with us dancing inside them. Oh, she's an easy one, they mumbled. She'll look and she'll listen, and she'll give us her words, her lovely own words. Oh, she'll sing with us again before the year is over.

Indeed, a year swiftly passed, and that future mother of five was going about her new wifely chores, with the Winds humming mildly about her. She had made her deal. Such a good deal, really, when you come to think of it. What was an arch of an eyebrow, after all? What a slight price for the pleasant composure she could now flaunt forever. And if you had tried talking to her about it, or if you had reminded her of those fond dreams she had forsaken, dreams of true love, love everlasting, all-abiding, why, she'd have that arch of an eyebrow all ready for you, wouldn't she? One of the clever, that's what she was now, and the mark on her brow was as clear as pain.

As for the whisper she had so rashly voiced, it was quite forgotten by now, of course it was, who would ever remember such a brief, fleeting whisper, why, the moment the ring slipped on her finger the whole thing slipped out of her mind. And if she ever felt a stab of yearning, if a glimmering snatch of desire sped through her heart, well, the Winds were always there to comfort her with their liquid, languid lisp, snatching up those dismal words: It will do, it will do.

And yet, even as she repeated those words—"It will do, it really will"—that arch of an eyebrow was there to mock her.

But a year did indeed pass, and as will happen to many a contented wife, Winds or no Winds, she now held in her arms a beautiful baby girl. Oh Joy, Oh Bliss, Oh Pride of her Eye, lovely little baby, lovely little arms, little legs, oh those lovely, lovely wide eyes looking at her, so empty of knowledge. So she hugged her newborn, and with a sigh of greatest satisfaction she said, "Oh, you doll, you sweet, I'll name you Liora, and you'll be the loveliest, loveliest girl ever. Mommy will love you to pieces, little one. And you'll love your Mommy. Always."

It was then, just then, that she felt a stab of fear—of course she did. How could she help it? She was such a young mother after all. Only her fear was a bit too bitter, her motherly arms just a touch too timid, her hands just a bit too quick to search for the mirror on the table beside her. And when she looked in the mirror she saw the fear in her eyes, clad, as always by now, with the sheen of the Loveless. Dread was creeping all through her bones. What if she wouldn't, what if the baby wouldn't, what if none of it would really, really do?

"No need for fear," whispered that flutey voice she knew so well by now, "No need to worry about this little one.

"We will show you the way," murmured the Winds, "just listen to our song."

And they taught her the Lullaby of the Loveless, a gentle tune of peril and retreat. How soothing it was, how comforting: for though it told of heartbreak and betrayal, it also told of sheltered homes and smooth, unruffled lakes, where pain could never reach you. That sudden chill had let go of her now, and she was smiling the new-mother smile, full of starry promise and delighted hope. And as she fell asleep, with her lovely daughter in arms, she quickly promised to sing her that song every evening, just after sunset, when the shadows were long.

And the Winds? What did they promise?

To protect her and hers forever.

"No pain shall ever touch her little heart," they promised.

"She shall love you forever," they promised.

"And she shall have a gift of her very own on her tenth birthday.

"Just sing her the song."

So she did. She sang her that lullaby every evening, when the shadows were long. "Hush little baby," she sang, "Mama will show you the safest land."

And the girl grew to that slithery tune, and she was told time and again that a gift would be hers some day, a gift that would keep her from any harm, ever.

And so they came, one after the other, Liora, Lenore, Layla, and Lihi, all wide-eyed and clear of heart, all held by arms that were never tired: this young bride, who had become a young wife and then a young mother, she was all set by now. She would keep her end of the bargain, she would sing them their songs, and gifts would be bestowed on them all. And that strange chill every time she held one of her newborns, well, she had gotten used to it, hadn't she? "It's just a pinch of silly nothing," she'd say as she smiled at herself in the mirror. And the Wind smiled right back in her eye.

And if her mouth was a bit tighter after the first child, and if her hands became a bit heavier after the second; and if her cheeks drooped with forgotten memories when Layla was born; and if anxiety finally came to settle in her eyes— well, it became a mother with four little girls on her hands, none but a fool would expect anything else. A baby's bath needed a firm hand; a motherly scold could use that pursed mouth. Any glimmers of past wishes and dreams were very few by now, and when she looked about her, when she saw her lovely cluster of daughters, a calm pride filled her heart just as well as anything she might ever have hoped for. Liora, Lenore, Layla, and Lihi, such lovelies, such pretties, all truly provided for by their devoted mother, each with a gift that would come in due time.

"Well, some of us are lucky. But no one's as lucky as me," the mother would say to herself every morning as she quickly glanced in the mirror, tying up her hair. "Look at us. Not one tear, not one sorrow, not a moment of pain. What a blessed household it is really, and all thanks to the good Winds."

Blessed household? Deaf, deaf household! A household asleep to the tune of that dread lullaby, a house where Loveless Winds mumbled nasty, greedy words from dawn to dusky dusk, and no one even noticed. "All ours, all ours to fondle, all ours to sing with, they will all be ours," hummed the Winds.

And if the shutters creaked ever so often, well, Mommy said it was such an old, charming house—just enough to suit them, charming as they all were.

The little sisters never even knew the Winds by their true name, nor did they know what it was that the Loveless Winds would give them.

But they learned that Lullaby of Dread by heart.

And they all received their gifts, just as promised.

Oh, dearest, what gifts these were! Golden medicine to fix any pain, vanishing cream to smooth out all sorrow, a bag of smiles for all occasions, and a bracelet of seven charms, to do away with any little disturbance at all.

It was on this very day, the day when Lihi turned ten, the day she was given that bracelet that could do away with the tiniest trouble, that the mother looked at herself in the mirror yet again. And while she had done this often over the years, she had always settled for a hasty snatch of a glance. But this time she looked for quite a while. Of course she did. She was a mother of four grown girls now: she needed some reflection.

She found it hard to believe at first. Those lines of doubt just above her ever-raised eyebrow, the dense bloating of her hands, that rigid line of a mouth, and the cheeks, so fallen, the eyes, so jittery.

A moment of reckoning: that's what she'd come to. Such moments do not abound in the Land of the Loveless: too hurtful, that's why. Yet a moment of reckoning it was, and it filled her with unspeakable woe.

But it also made her shut her eyes and think silently just for once, so none could hear.

Look at me, she thought, look how dearly I've been made to pay. And all for what? Liora can fix anything with her medicine, she has no use for me or for anyone else; Lenore's smooth face chills me to the bone, Layla's smile is so careless, and Lihi—she could probably charm me away whenever she likes. As for my husband . . . Well, what of him? He will do, he will, but only for so much. And it never was very much at all.

Just one more, she thought. Just one more chance, one more lovely, I know she will smooth out this awful face of mine. It will be different this time, surely it will. I'm not so young anymore, not so fearful, not at all. This one will be my luck-child, my star, this one shall be a child of love.

And she looked at herself again, very earnestly.

"Ooooh! What love?!" mocked the Winds in the mirror. "We've done away with all that years ago, haven't we." They were not so gentle by now, of course they weren't, not after years and years of undisturbed dominion. This was no novice to be lured and trapped, this was a woman who had heard the Loveless tune to the point of near-deafness, a woman who had given them all her words to play with freely. Cruel shrieks were quite all right by now.

"Just one last child," she pleaded—with herself, really. "Surely there's some love left for just one more!"

Now you must remember this, dearest, for it may come in handy: no matter how hard a Loveless Wind blows, you may always defy it. Plug your ears, dearest, use your fingers, use wax, and the Wind will have no hold on you. And it was just this the mother decided to do. The best years of her life had been played out to the tune of those shrill Loveless Winds—she would take her leap now, just for once, and have the star-child of her dreams. "A little one shall be born to me," she said out loud. "No Wind shall ever touch her heart, no Loveless word will ever tempt her."

And because twenty chill years had passed, and because she wished so hard, so well, so late in the day, a Love-child was born.

Luna was born on a fey and gray November day, when the Winds were singing a simple autumn tune. How gladly that mother of five looked at her baby. How fondly she played with those little toes. All coos and smiles she was, all coos and smiles. And did she feel that pinch of silly nothing, that chill, that fear, that shivery dread that had made her promise away so much? No she didn't. Not anymore. It's happened, she proudly thought, this is my star-child, my luck-child, the child who has smoothed out my face with love.

"Why don't you check for yourself," a wisp of a Wind lisped at her ear, "there's a mirror right by your bed."

"I needn't a mirror, thank you," the wise mother of five replied, remembering only too well her first encounter with those wily Winds.

"Oh you don't, do you," the Wind replied. "You're quite sure of your little miracle, aren't you? The baby to end all babies, the lucky star of love to shine on your aging forehead. Why would you look in the mirror, why indeed? Certainly such a sweet creature has smoothed you out just as smooth as chocolate pie . . ."

On it went, on and on. She couldn't help but listen to that voice. And the mirror, so close to her, why shouldn't she look? One look would calm her little inkling of a doubt, just one look would give her the assurance she needed to chase that vile Wind away. Just a peek, really.

This is the truth, dearest: none of us will ever know What If. What if she hadn't. Because she did. And once she glanced into that polished mirror, well, there they were, all of them: the arch of her eyebrow, the pinch of her mouth, the sag of her cheek, and the shiver in her eye. And she had to admit it: her hands, holding that mirror, felt as heavy as ever.

Bitter, bitter woe! Dear, dear grief! She couldn't take her eyes off that mirror now, and the Winds, how they shrieked and howled, how they tossed her bitterest words right back at her. "You fool, you proud, stupid fool, whatever made you think you could stop us from singing? Look at your face, just look at it, what made you think you could wish away such a face?

"As for that love-child of yours, well, we shall see about it, won't we? We'll see about it indeed. She shall be made to listen, she shall be made to sit up and take notice, just you wait and see!"

Now the Winds can sing many a song, they can sing songs of despair so dry it would drive you out of your wits to hear them. And that poor fool of a mother, that vain mother who had used up every bit of hope still left in her cautious heart, she had listened once too often. "Never let the Winds tempt you," she quickly said to her little daughter, "don't ever let them touch your heart." And with that last loving wish, her heart was ravished forever, with no words left but the bitter-smart words of the Loveless.

With no more hope of reflection, ever.

With no shred of faith, no trace of regret.

All hollowed out.

But the baby, that little baby in her arms, the baby that had been wished for so truly, the baby blessed with such a fervent, last wish, she just looked up at her mother with dark, bottomless eyes, eyes of love unending.

A luck-child. A star-child. A love-child indeed.

And so she grew, lovely little Luna, Luna the last, the loveliest, sweet little Luna, moaning in her cradle, rocked to sleep by bitter Winds, her curls tossed about in a painful jumble. Oh she heard those Winds very well, she could feel them grazing her face, she could see them shrouding her mother with a dark cloak of despair, only she was so tiny, so fresh to the world, she couldn't even name them. But anyone who came to visit, anyone who brought flowers for the new mother of five, would wonder at that little baby moaning in her cradle, so tiny, so lovely, yet tossing about in unspoken pain.

"It's the Wind," she said as soon as she started to speak. "It hurts me inside."

"Too delicate," that's what they all said. "She'll muddle through, for sure." Too delicate. Why else would she mind the Winds so much? After all, these were gentle, mellow Winds, who never broke a thing, who at their hardest only turned a page or two of the book they happened to be reading, who always had such smooth tunes, made just for them.

So the Winds continued their playful howling, their chilly fondling and dancing, and there was only one to feel it in that blessed, deaf household, one so gentle, so soft, sweet, sad little Luna, all alone in that house where even lullabies were loveless, her sisters quite grown now, each and every one of them with her own gift, and that mother of five—no longer frightened, no longer doubtful, all hollowed out, watching her little one doubling up as the Winds stormed about her.

"They hurt me so," the child insisted. "They make me hurt all over."

"Hush little baby," replied the mother. "Hush little baby," she sang. "Mama will show you the safest land."

It was the only song she remembered by now.

But the girl wouldn't hush—that lullaby all the sisters had grown to, it gave her nightmares, it made her throw up with fear. The Winds' soft whispers seemed like shrieks to her; in their cautious tones she heard veiled mockery, and in their light touch she sensed a forbidding chill.

And she'd hide in her corner at the slightest whisper of a breeze.

As for the Winds, they never gave up, they howled with endless fury at this child, who never once heeded their words.

Simple, sweet little Luna, whose only wish, ever, was to feel the sweet touch of love on her cheek.

And strangely enough, she did.

The four sisters would see the little one moaning in her high-chair, they'd see her look for her shattered dolls in the garden, and something stirred within them, some softness never called for before, a shock of mercy, a stab of sorrow no Wind could make them forget.

And it was Layla who said, "See how little she is, see how she hurts. We must take care of her."

Which they did. They truly did. Only they had such ways! "Have some of this," Liora would say, holding out a spoonful of golden soothing drops, but Luna wouldn't. Those drops were so sour on her sweet, simple tongue.

"Put some of this where it aches," said Lenore, holding out some of her cream, which could smooth away any trace of a hurt. But Luna couldn't. That magic cream singed her skin like a shower of dry ice.

And when Layla suggested one of her smiles, a good, cheerful tip-of-the-nose smile, even then Luna winced with displeasure. "It doesn't look nice on me at all," she said in her sweet sing-song of a voice, "Look, it makes my eyes look even darker!" And it did, oh how it did, those dark, bottomless eyes where no Loveless Wind could ever hide, those eyes which could never reflect a thing, eyes that let you sink all the way in, the eyes of true love.

"Try my bracelet," Lihi finally said, "Perhaps you could charm away the pain."

"I hate those dings and dongs," said little Luna, "they sound so nasty." And they did, they certainly did— brief peals of indifference, little echoes of the Winds' haughty tunes, painful music to such tender ears.

"Couldn't they comfort her at all?" you ask, "Wasn't there anything at all they could do for her?"

There was. Indeed there was, and the learning of it was their saving. A little tender lullaby made up just for her, with not a word of torment; the softest of tones, the mildest of hugs, all found in some hidden corner of their hearts. Layla would tell Luna little stories, stories with no Winds or monsters, stories all fluff and happiness, which she would never, ever forget.

"There's four of us to raise her," said Layla, who loved Luna best of all, who looked into her eyes and and found herself dreaming of distance.

"There's four of us, and we must shelter her from those Winds," she said.

And they tried, they truly did. With special screens and shutters, with incantations dreamt up just for her. For

Luna was indeed the love-child, and she could touch the coldest of hearts.

But they never quite believed her, and they never used that name she had for the Winds.

"Those Winds are evil," she'd say, but no one in that house would listen.

"The Winds are our friends," the mother explained to her with the tiredest of voices. "The Winds will take care of you, they love you, how could you think they're evil? Why would they want to hurt you at all?"

But Luna, sweet little Luna, all marshmallow and cream, she had that one ounce of defiance, that little grain of childish stubbornness really, that made her insist. "They're evil, Mama, they want to blow right through us and never have to stop. They're evil, Mama. They're loveless."

Now if there's one thing the Loveless Winds truly hate, it's being called by their name. Indeed, the Winds have many other names for themselves, such as the Winds of Caution, the Winds of Temperance, and best of all, the Winds of Wisdom. So whenever the Winds heard little Luna speak of them, they'd roil with fury. Insulted, that's what they were. Truly and thoroughly insulted. And they weren't ones to take insult slightly. Oh how they howled about her, through her, wilder and wilder, making her shriek with pain, chasing her on the gloomiest of paths, tormenting her night and day with their bitter reproach.

But she never let them touch her heart, and she never had any words to lend them.

As she grew, the pain became sharper, and her words, they became darker. "They'll hollow you out," she cried again and again. "They'll turn your hearts into a barren desert, they'll have you all dry and loveless, just like them. They'll have you glued to that mirror, listening to their song. And after you've listened long enough, after you've given away one dear hope after another, then you'll be theirs forever, then you'll sing their song for the rest of your life. Don't you see how they crave words for their horrible tune?

"The Loveless tune will echo all over you," she shrieked, herself as wild as any Wind could wish to be. "You'll be their instrument, that's what, and they'll play out their song on the broken strings of your heart!"

Well, it couldn't go on like that. Not forever. That girl had grown so wild, so careless with her words, and the Winds, they were so desperate by now, frantic with worry, never thinking of her anymore, only hoping the other sisters wouldn't listen too closely to her prophecies of gloom.

Luna died on the day of her twelfth birthday, torn apart by the most vindictive of Winds, a great Typhoon that ripped her up inside, burst and scattered her like the sparkliest of sparkly bubbles, did away with her like a fleeting shimmer on a dark lake.

That's it? Not one shred of mercy? Not a trace of justice? How vicious could those vicious Winds be? Surely, you ask, even in those valleys of lovelessness some comfort would remain?

Well, yes.

Somewhat.

If you were willing to pay for it.

Dearly, my dearest. Very dearly.

It was the evening of the day on which they buried Luna. That crushed mother of five was not to be reckoned with, and the father too had wasted away many years ago. The four sisters sat together, huddled up in the dark home of their childhood, wondering what they'd do now that their beloved sister was dead, how they'd live their lives now that those sweet earnest eyes were gone forever.

"Perhaps she was right," said Layla. "Perhaps she was right all along. She did say those Winds were evil."

"She said so many things, that poor little one," replied Liora, who had left home quite a few years ago and already had two charming little children of her own.

"She *was* a bit fanciful," said smooth Lenore, who was living in New York at the time and had come home for the funeral.

But Layla and Lihi, who had been right there by Luna's side, who had seen her daily torment right to the very end, they had their own thoughts.

"She could have been right," Layla insisted, without even starting to think what that might mean.

And only Lihi, who had always liked Layla best of all, only she said, "Perhaps." The older two sisters, the mild and the daring, they just sat there, their mouths as sad as could be, but empty of any reproach, their cautious hearts quite affectionate, but hardly as full as you'd wish them.

Silently they looked at each other, seeking each other's eyes, searching for answers that had never been there.

And so they sat there, all so alike, so pretty, all so young really, only some were younger than others. More impressionable, if you like. More likely to jump to conclusions, which isn't always such a bad thing to do.

Now the Winds, they were listening carefully. Wondering just a bit, had they gone too far? Wondering also, what would be required to keep those four lovelies as close as could be. What they would have to pay. Wondering, just the same, what they could get in return. For the Winds, dearest, have their own peculiar way of haggling, and whenever they're made to pay for something, they ask for something else in return. A bonus, if you like. A coupon of sorts, for future use.

"We can bring her back," the Winds sang tenderly, with the softest of murmurs.

"She can come to see you," they promised.

And the sisters, they listened. Of course they did, how could they help it, when that lump of nothingness sat so heavily on their hearts?

A deal.

A bargain.

How like the Winds to offer a deal on the bleakest of days.

It was a good bargain, they all agreed, as easy as plucking an eyebrow. "Just follow our Rule," the Winds sang. "Learn our Rule, and your sister will be allowed to visit you ever so often."

Oh, what a Rule. So simple, so brief, such an easy

task really, even more so for anyone who had grown up with the Loveless Lullaby in her ear. What a Rule! So simple, so bitter, only the cleverest of Loveless Winds could dream it up.

Just this:

"Never love a man while he lies asleep."

Yes dearest, just this.

So they promised away that which seemed so easy to promise, never once thinking they would come to regret it.

And if they did, later on, there was always a caressing Wind who sang of prudence, and made their eyes shine with the pride of the calm.

Until now, after all these years, when Layla found the scooter.

A scooter that seemed to ride over and above any Wind.

5
even in Paris,
even at twenty

So there she was, the whole world just lying at her feet. How confusing, embarrassing even, for one little housewife (which is what she really was, wasn't it? For if her arms were cramped it was only with laundry and baby-carrying, and it's cramps that count, when you want to know what someone really is.)

There she was indeed, her scooter accounted for, her one trip glibly smoothed over, all stretched out of shape by so many imaginations, it almost seemed possible to forget how sad it had really been.

"When are you going on another trip, Layla," her sisters would ask, each with her own little tones, some mocking, some glad, but all of them small.

"When are you going on another trip, Layla," the husband would ask, with a studied glance of casualness.

And the girls, too. Of course she had told the girls.

Disclosure wouldn't be full without telling the girls, so she did, one afternoon, as they raked the leaves under the pine tree—such a game, really, even that could still become a game. Oh she told them all right, with all the brightness Layla could put into words, "You know, sometimes, when no one's home, Mommy gets up on the scooter and flies all the way to Alaska!"

Now the girls, small though they were, were sure Mommy was just making it up. But Layla, our Layla, she felt so clever, she had finally smiled off Alaska, she had wrapped it up in that mommy-brightness which always made everything all right, which had made it all right for so long now, surely it could still do that, surely it could do away with that chill spell the mink had cast on her.

So she kept it up, and she even told them about a silly old mink hidden in an oak tree, all blind with snowy whiteness, and in this story Mommy had actually teased the old mink, she had told him just how blind and silly he was, and he had dug himself deeper in his hole, quite ashamed of himself.

There, that felt almost better!

And so, even though it seemed everyone was expecting her to take off again, Layla was full of excuses. "It's Liora's birthday next Saturday," she'd tell her sisters. "I can't really go before then," or else, "The child is sick again, so the scooter must wait." And so it went, on and on. It almost seemed as if she were hoping that the scooter would go all rusty again.

But it didn't.

Because, you see, many years ago, Layla had been granted a wish, and she had chosen well.

It was the day before her twentieth birthday. She was playing her flute in a metro station in Paris, her Indian scarf lying on the ground, ready for coins. She didn't play very well, but she had learned that this didn't really matter—people paid for the satisfaction of recognizing a tune. So she only played easy, familiar old songs, and sure enough, many tourists would stop for a moment, happy to stand there humming, just as one should in Paris. After about two hours she had quite a nice little amount of coins, so she packed in her flute, and put the scarf on her neck, and went straight off to the nearest museum. You see, she was quite serious-minded. Even in Paris. Even at twenty.

So in she went, very pleased with herself; and she walked very slowly, watched very thoroughly, wondering all the time why it was that she had to do all this alone.

It was after about an hour that the elf showed up. She was looking at some little Egyptian cats in a glass case when suddenly she noticed him walking around her. So she walked on, looking at his face through the glass. A sharp face it was, very bright, narrow eyes under thick, low eyebrows. He wore a dirty white shirt, with some kind of embroidery, loose cotton pants, and frayed slippers. She couldn't believe her good luck.

Three times Layla and the elf circled the cats, and then he spoke to her. "You play very well," he said. But she didn't say anything. She had never met an elf before, you see. And she was a bit confused about his feet—they were dirty, which she hadn't expected. But his words, they were so soft, his lips so red, his voice and his accent so other-worldly. So out they went. Serious-minded she was, and she knew very well that this mattered more than Egyptian cats.

Of course he chose a shady, green little corner in the park. They sat there for hours, saying just a few words at a time. She almost felt like a fairy herself. She could feel her eyes becoming brighter and brighter, her brow becoming higher and whiter. She couldn't believe how nice he was to her, saying such lovely things, especially about her hair.

But mostly he gazed at her, and she sat there, hoping to be admitted.

Suddenly he got up. He had to leave. However, he did promise to come again the next day. He even told her when and where he would meet her.

There she waited for him, and there he came, almost on time. She had borrowed some earrings and had found some perfume, and a brown T-shirt seemed to add a syl-van touch to her jeans. He embraced her—his arms quite strong, yet curiously light—but he wouldn't kiss her, even though she tried putting up her face several times.

"It's my birthday, you know," she said after a while.

It was then that the elf looked into her eyes with a gaze even brighter. "Then you must make a wish," he said. "What will it be?"

Now you see, even though Layla had longed to meet a fairy or someone of the wish-granting type ever since she was a child, she didn't have her answer ready. At the age of five she had the three wishes pat: long red hair, green eyes, and a dress all pink and lace. But by now she was twenty, and serious-minded, and she was given only one wish. She had no idea what to ask for, and was trying to smile the whole thing away, but he just kept gazing at her, expecting an answer.

She was almost upset. Here she was, having such a lovely, leisurely time with her very own elf, and suddenly he comes up with this serious, once-in-a-lifetime kind of proposition. A few answers came to her mind, but they all seemed too silly for this earnest elf. "Oh, I just wish to be happy," she said, smiling it all away.

"Happy" being such a simple word, as in happily ever after, a trickier word than Layla could have then guessed, as in happy with one's life, happy with one's lot, the whole messy lot of it—who could know what Layla meant by it? She certainly didn't.

Just as he vanished, she saw him look at her with his wonderful, warm, blue-eyed smile.

So you see, the scooter couldn't just rust and let her stay in her little house. It had to remain there, nice and ready, quietly commanding Layla to ride it again, to fly once more above the tree-tops with the wind in her hair.

But she was still serious-minded, our Layla, method-ical, one might say. She had to take care of that cold, doubtful little mink before she could do anything else. She couldn't go anywhere else before that taunting voice was silenced, once and for all. So, almost in spite of herself, she started preparing for her trip back to Alaska. I'll settle things with that nasty creature, she thought, and then I can go on wherever I like. She had really liked it, you see, this business of being Princess Layla of the Flying Scooter. "There's no stopping me now," she'd say to herself while walking the little corridors of her house, "if rust can become magic, if old scooters can fly, why, then I can become a princess." So she hunted up her treasure chest, and there she found her old Indian scarf. She even found the museum ticket, which she had kept all these years. And she found a little, white crochet bag to put them both in.

What else did she take with her, now that she was on her way to become a seasoned scooter-traveller? A small, three-colored rock, an African comb, the seven-charmed bracelet her younger sister had given her, and, of course, her father's old compass.

So, on a still summer night, when everyone was quite asleep in that little house, Layla flew back to Alaska. She took her little bag and got on her scooter, and it knew just where to go. She sat on it, her legs dangling down on both sides, her face quite white, her hair laughing about her.

Very slowly she got there, all silver with cold.

"Oh here you are again," the mink said. "Nothing has changed since the last time, you know.

"There's really nothing to see," the mink repeated, cold as ever. That's the way of the mink, don't you know, a narrow, friendless way.

But Layla, our own Layla, why did she stand there listening?

Because he could do that, the little mink; because he could make her feel there was so much he knew, even though he said so little. And perhaps it was just because he said so little, leaving so much to be guessed, leaving blanks of such hollow emptiness, such voids really, so easy to fill with despair.

He's doing it again, she thought, feeling how sad her cheeks were becoming. It's that voice of his, really, it chills my bones and freezes my fingers. Indeed, there was something about this voice, something so familiar, so annoying, it made Layla hold up her chin, even here.

"I'm fed up with you," she said, with an imperious toss of her hair.

"Oh are you," replied the mink, a thin smile on his face. "And what, may I ask, is it that you object to?"

This was where she started to stammer, knowing all the while that stammering was not a princessly thing to do. Which only made the stammering worse, right? "It's the snow, really, and all this cold whiteness," she said. "Don't you have geysers in Alaska? Don't you have any cities? Or forests? Aren't there any attractions at all?"

"Next thing, you'll be asking for castles," he said, baring a few of his sharp little teeth.

"Well why not? A castle would be quite nice. One does see them in other places when one's sight-seeing."

"I know all about you," said the mink. "What you really want is a bloody Prince."

"No I don't," she insisted, gathering back just a bit of courage. "It isn't that at all. I've come for the sights."

There she was, standing in front of that oak tree, nothing but snow all around her. What a brave little Layla, really, miles and miles away from home, clutching her crochet bag, arguing with this irksome little stranger as if no one had ever told her that arguing was quite out of the question. Because it is, isn't it? You wouldn't just start complaining about the sights to the first Alaskan you ever met, especially if he happened to be a talking mink, which is, after all, a rather exceptional kind of Alaskan. But Layla put on her scarf, wrapped it round her head three times, quite the princess after all. And being a princess, she felt a royal bit of anger creeping up from her frozen toes all the way to her eyebrows. "You have vexed me," she said, and just managed to stifle a surprised, scared little giggle. But she was becoming a bit taller right then, and the mink wasn't quite sure what to say.

"I haven't come all this way just to be vexed by a nasty creature like you," she continued. She was getting used to this new way of putting a sentence. She felt she could really come to like it.

"Were I in the mood," she said, "I would have you skinned for a souvenir. But you are too loathsome even for that. So away with you, and fast!"

And then she shook her bracelet—the wonderful, seven-charmed bracelet her younger sister had given her. How it rang, that lovely golden trinket. You could hear spring with each chime, you could feel warmth spreading all over, to the frozen tip of your nose. Twice Layla shook her bracelet, and—*ding!*—the mink disappeared—*dong!*—there went the oak tree too.

And *ding*—Alaska was full of flowers? And *dong*—there was the castle, turrets, moat, and all?

But of course not. Alaska remained as white as ever, ding-dong or no ding-dong.

If you think about it very carefully, Alaska was actually whiter than before, now that the mink and the oak tree were gone.

Still, Layla stood there undaunted. Now I'm truly Layla the Princess, she thought, Layla the mink-conqueror. And with quite a certain step, considering, she started her search.

So what was it she wanted to find? Quite a minkish question, don't you think? She just walked ahead, humming a little tune, making up the words as she went along, swinging her arms to her heart's content. Because she wasn't really hard to please, no matter what the mink had thought.

"But did she look for a Prince or didn't she?" you ask.

Well, that's a question that must remain unanswered, mustn't it, she being so careful and all. Let's put it this way: just for the moment, a nice, open stretch of snow was quite enough.

How surprised she was, then, when her first real adventure actually started.

This is what happened:

Her arm-swinging, soft-humming walk was so pleasant, that she walked for quite a while before noticing that the scooter, too, had disappeared. Now that's strange, she thought. You see, she wasn't sure whether she had come a long way, or whether the scooter had just been donged out of sight, along with the mink and the oak tree. There she was, all by herself, without even a scooter to take her home. "This isn't an adventure," she complained out loud. "This is your average nightmare."

"No it isn't," said the elf, "it's a totally genuine adventure, and you, dear Layla, are our heroine."

Now Layla just stood there, her mouth quite open, her eyes darting all over the place. "What are you doing here?" she finally said, in her palest, dizziest voice. "And who's 'we'?"

"I missed you, dearest Layla, it's been such a long time," he replied, ignoring her second question—it was a secret, you see, and Layla still looked like someone who could change her mind about things, maybe even betray an old friend or two.

"But why didn't you come to see me all these years and how did you know I was here and why haven't you helped me at all till now?" Layla started to cry. This lasted for a while, she being so tired and confused, and the elf just stood there, in that way elves have, quite easy and relaxed, without even having to shift his weight or anything, just standing, as though his legs themselves were patiently waiting for Layla's tears to stop.

"Oh you lovely, silly, lovely little Layla, you never even asked," he finally said, "And I do hate to intrude on a happy home."

She didn't say anything now, and neither did the elf. He just took her by the hand, and showed her a lovely little path that lay hidden between the snowy hills. Sheltered it was, just wide enough for the two of them to walk on pleasantly. "Where are you taking me?" she asked. But he just smiled and said, "You wanted some castles, didn't you?" And so they went on walking for, oh, who knows how long? It was all so white and dazzling one couldn't really tell.

By now Layla's hair was so long she could feel it softly swishing against her ankles. And, would you believe it, its color had changed the moment she saw the elf, and was now quite silvery, breezily floating about her, making her feel more delicious than ever. "Layla the lovely," she said to herself, humming a gentle tune to the words, which she repeated again and again with great pleasure. The elf's hand was light and dry, cool against her warm skin. He was wearing a robe, white with silver embroidery, and his feet were bare.

"Why aren't we cold?" she remembered to ask.

"Why have you become so lovely?" he asked in reply, a light smile shimmering over his eyes.

Now they saw, standing there, just in front of them, the desired castle. A real castle it was, turrets and flags, a dozen each, and a moat all around it. Layla was so confused, she just clung to the elf and asked, "All this just for me?"

"But only for as long as you like," he answered, and vanished again. That's the kind of elf he was, you see. Sprightly.

So she crossed the drawbridge and walked in very carefully, the silence heavy about her. Along the somber hall, past mirrors and dark columns, over thick carpets she went, wondering about the servants, afraid to call out. She walked through the magnificent halls, so tiny under the vast ceilings she almost felt like a child. The place seemed quite empty, there wasn't even a trace of sound, no quick, far-away footstep. Looking about her she noticed there wasn't even any furniture. What a strange castle it is, she thought. I wonder, was it really put here just for me? It did cross her mind, that while she had mentioned a castle in her conversation with the mink, she hadn't mentioned any king or queen. I actually told him I wasn't looking for a prince, she said, and had you been there, you might have heard an edge of irritation in her voice.

So there she was, Layla of the Flying Scooter, feeling, oh, just a bit silly, with that big castle all to herself, wondering what else she could have hoped for, now that hope seemed such a simple, do-it-yourself sort of thing. You see, it had been so many years since Layla stopped hoping, she wasn't very good at it anymore.

It was the big hopes that went first. Those charmed visions of a sunlit house full of friends and laughter; chatty, thrilling, evenings of clever talk; and of course love, love against all odds, love everlasting, overwhelming, love healing every blemish on her life. The radiance of recognition—*dong!* Starry desert nights—*ding!* A gorgeous figure—*dong!* Gentle, smiling care—*ding!* Very soon the smaller hopes followed. Good-morning kisses, family day-trips, balloons for her birthday. Birthdays were hardest to forgive.

But in the mornings, when she woke up with that heavy feeling upon her, she'd blame it all on her dreams and get up as fast as ever. And then she'd hug her girls and think, When they grow up we'll see, maybe there still will be time for hoping.

So here she was now, pacing those empty halls with large, restless steps, quite the vexed princess after all. Well it does seem to be mine, she said after a while. I may as well use it. It could be my thinking-corner. There's certainly nothing here to stop me from thinking. Definitely not the noise, she giggled, in a very cozy sort of way. She was a giggling sort of Layla, you see, only she hadn't had very much of a chance for giggling lately.

There she sat, right in the middle of the biggest hall, and had herself some thoughts. After all, there was quite a lot to think, or even just wonder about, and so much room to do it in.

Now Layla, it must be said, was no great thinker, not in any way that could really fill up a whole thinking-corner. I wonder about the elf, she thought. Which was followed by, I wonder about the scooter, and immediately afterwards, Shall I go home again?

Of course she knew she'd be going home. That didn't take very much thinking. Those lovely girls were waiting—who knows for how long? But this led her to the following thought, which had, as its subject, her husband of seven years. "Do I or don't I?" she asked, and "Does he, or not?" She was a simple-minded kind of Layla, you see, so that every thought was no more than a deep abyss to be crossed—or not. Now the question of love had been settled a long time ago, you do remember that. But this was the kind of thinking she was good at, carefully touching a thought, letting it quickly drop, picking it up after some time and looking at it again as though she had never seen it before. This she did now, immediately answering herself, Oh well, love seems to be a bit of a tall order right now; the question is, what to do next. Sitting here, in all this splendrous vastness, she couldn't quite imagine herself back in that house of hers. She didn't like the emptiness of the palace, or the quiet, echoing halls; but it did occur to her that where there was one elf there could be more, and indeed, such a wondrous place couldn't remain empty forever.

"The issue really is, am I a princess or not," she slowly said to herself. She was trying to be methodical, you see.

Now this wasn't an easy question, not really. It was very obvious to Layla that she hadn't been a princess till now. There hadn't been any golden cradle or silver slippers or charmed frogs—nothing to even hint at hidden royalty. No special birthmarks either, no finding in the forest, no starry cloak or swaddling clothes. But since I have a palace that is all my own, and since I have a flying scooter, it seems that I have become a princess after all, she concluded, quite promptly. Which led her to a happy train of imaginary ballrooms and curls and dresses, all covered with diamonds. Not a very serious kind of thinking, not at all, but ever so pleasant. Especially that part about the little crown on her head, nothing overwhelming, just a delicate silver band with some fine stones sparkling on it.

It isn't enough, she very soberly told herself after a while. A scooter and an empty palace in the middle of all this snow really aren't enough, not if I'm to be a real princess. Why, here I am, all alone in this strange place, with no one to talk to. I might as well go home. So she got up and stretched her legs, ready for the return trip.

We'll see, she told herself. Maybe I am and maybe I'm not, it may take some time to know. And in a way, she felt quite proud of herself, having had so many deep, conclusive thoughts all at once.

She knew just what to do now. "I want my scooter," she said very calmly. And indeed, there it was, all sparkly and ready to go.

Back, back above the snow, above the endless skies, back through unspun dreams, through vague wishes, through veils of warm darkness, and there she was, under the pine tree.

She could do it, you see, walk in, kiss her girls, start the rice cooking. The husband wasn't home, which made it so much simpler. I'm a secret sort of princess, she told herself, a cooking and cleaning princess, which is a very special sort. But she only dusted a bit and never touched the mop and the bucket. That seemed a bit too much by now.

And when the husband returned she gave him dinner. Pampered he was, with creamed macaroni; hugged all over, wasn't he.

At night, in bed, she held his face and looked very deeply into his eyes. Was he or wasn't he? Could he or not? She had this trick, our Layla, she could see just a bit of a thing at a time, just the bit she chose. Now she chose his eyes. *Ding!*—went the face, *Dong!*—went the room. It was just Layla and a set of brown eyes, they could be anyone's, really. Deep, deep in she went. Searching, it seemed, that gaze of hers, scientific, speculative, probing. Deeper and deeper: artistic, poetic. Inventive. Maybe he could. Maybe she could. "Your eyes are so kind," she said, and off she went, telling him all about who he really was: reminding him, that's what she called it. She never said "Prince," but had you been there, you would have heard the word hovering right above her quick, gushing sentences.

So what did he do? Was he charmed? Did he soar up and away on her winged tongue?

Confused, that's what he was. And tired. But mostly confused. Just a bit alarmed, too. What did she want, this bright-eyed woman, this restless wife of his? What was she trying to make him do? Where was she trying to take him? And who, on earth, was she talking about? You see, he could hear that hovering, unspoken word just as clearly as you can. And princedom had never even been part of his dreams.

But Layla, how could she know? Smart though she was, it never entered her wildest thoughts that a person could give up on princedom. So she kept up the talking, night after night, and the gazing too, and of course she was so moved there were tears all over the bed. There she was, reminding him of his birthright. Surely he would claim it once he saw the light.

6
earl grey,
please

It was just ten days later that Liora had her annual transplant-party. Layla always liked Liora's transplant-parties—just the five of them, all dressed in white, sipping Liora's delicious mint tea, talking about the mysteries of the heart.

And indeed it was mysterious.

You see, twelve years ago, Liora had been given a new heart. The old one, it was so tired and bruised, the doctors all agreed it had to come out. So out it went, on a cold February afternoon, and in came a new, wonderfully calm heart, so healthy and strong she could hardly recall what life had been like before.

And the old one, they just put it in a bright glass jar, soaked it in smelly water that would keep it fresh forever. Only it kept on beating, that old heart, all by itself, in that smelly jar. Everyone was quite embarrassed at first.

Doctors and nurses and specialists too, they'd come and look at it, and look some more, staring really, and then they'd say, "This must be stopped."

But they didn't know how.

And when they told Liora about it she just said, "That's perfectly fine, I know just what to do. You must let me have it."

So they did, even though it was against the rules: no one was supposed to keep their old heart once they got a new one. Too confusing, that's why.

But Liora, she wasn't one to be confused. She just held the jar in her hand, and looked at that old heart of hers, beating away, counting its memories, and she said, "You'll be good for my garden." And as soon as she got well, which was in no time at all, she took it home with her. In it went, on a cold rainy night, that old, restless, stubborn heart, right where it belonged, beneath the rose and mint bushes.

"I always meant to ask you, did you bury it with or without the jar?" said Lenore.

"I wonder if it's still beating down there," Lihi said while drinking her tea.

"Could it still feel any love?" Layla quietly mused.

But Luna, she was as silent as ever.

"Without," replied Liora. "And I don't know about the beating. As for love, that's quite beside the point, isn't it? I don't know, and I certainly have no need for it. And this new heart of mine, it works so well, it has never even had to trouble itself about love."

They all nodded, but some nods were smaller than

others, and Luna, she didn't nod at all. She just sat there, her face so blank there was nothing but sadness left to see. But Luna was always silent, especially when it came to love. Remember, she now sat there by courtesy of the Loveless Winds, as a special privilege, to be revoked whenever, to be withdrawn if ever any one of them broke the Loveless Rule. So she could only sit there, silent, and hope her sisters would be dealt with kindly. And when she was asked she said, "I can only tell you about Lovelessness. It hurts."

"The other hurts too," Layla told her.

"Nothing hurts me," Liora reminded them.

But when Luna looked at her, with those bleak, dark eyes, she added, almost furiously, "Spare me your eyes, will you. I do love my children, all six of them. All the tiny lot of them. And my husband, why, he's just another child, isn't he?" And they all sat there smiling, affectionately recalling the husband's minute hands and feet.

"Love is all very fine," Liora added, encouraged by their smiles, "but what about meals? One couldn't really do anything if one went about loving all day. It's all right when you're a girl, with nothing else on your hands. But now—my sweet little husband, he needs his meals cooked just right and his clothes pressed tight. And at night, do you know how many little kisses behind the ear he needs just to get on top of me? And in the mornings, why, there's cereal to mix, my extra-brittle one, to keep him brave for the rest of the day.

"Now love, love as in Love, that would be something else, wouldn't it? I'd just lie there in bed, moaning, quite careless, wouldn't I? Measuring his little prick every night, to see if it will do. Looking for flowers every weekend. Why, he'd have to do the double-vaulted backflip every morning, if it were all about Love."

And she sat back, snug in her big white shawl, gently smiling at them. There was no denying it, she looked so healthy, her eyes so clear, her skin positively translucent, her body faintly smelling of lavender. "Have some more tea," she said, but our Layla, she was careful now, she remembered times when the husband had had larger feet, when Liora's skin had been quite ordinary. "Could I have some Earl Grey, please?" she asked discreetly. Liora frowned, but she brought her the regular tea, and Layla felt so relieved. You see, all those years since her marriage, Layla had been drinking Liora's soothing mint tea; now she didn't want to be soothed anymore. And she definitely didn't want to get any smaller. She wished her older sister would have more than just one tea, more than one sort of medicine. Why, if she had some sparkly, sizzling kind of tea, she thought, I'd be glad to have some; I'd even give some to that husband of mine. But Liora hadn't any such tea. Sizzling had been quite out of the question for many years now as far as she was concerned.

So there they sat, the mild, the daring, the young, and the sad. And Layla. Layla the searching, the questioning. Layla the hoping. Princess Layla of the Hopeful Scooter, she giggled to herself.

Now Layla had many a smile, I have said, and her sisters knew them all. But this quiet giggle, this Earl Grey business, what on earth did it mean? So they asked her.

And she smiled and said, "Oh, I was thinking about my scooter," which they all knew about already, remember?

But did she mention the castle?

And what about the elf?

And this new royal aspect of hers, did she say even a word about that?

Indeed she didn't.

Once I'm all done, she told herself, they'll know. There's no point in telling them something they won't believe.

So she said nothing about her new friend or her new possessions. She just told them about the snow, and the mink, and they all said it sounded nasty and spooky and cold.

"Who would have thought," said Lenore, "who would have thought you'd go for all that snow? What on earth are you looking for in that white desert? If it's restlessness that's troubling you, why don't you come over to my place? There's quite a lot going on there." And would you believe it, she winked. A lewd, fat wink, which hid a harsh, cyanide eye. "All you really need is a good fuck," she sweetly said, "I've been saying that for years. Then you can stop all this crazy Mink and Snow stuff." It was her turn to giggle now, a cold, quick giggle. "M&S, I don't believe it. You should try and reverse them some time."

This was going just a bit far, wasn't it. This wasn't quite the kind of talk you'd expect on a transplant party, not the sort of thing white-clad sisters should hear, let alone talk about. But remember, Lenore's eyes were cyanide-blue now, and they all knew anything could happen when her eyes changed, when she dropped all that sweet violet so many men had drowned in.

So Liora said, "Go rinse your mouth. And do something about your eyes. Right now!" And Lenore, she obeyed her older sister; that was one of their little rules.

Soon the party was over. It had to be. For this is another thing you should know: whenever any one of the sisters went too far, it was time for everyone to go home. They didn't believe in it, you see, this idea of distance.

Only Layla, who day-dreamed of snow all day, she thought, I wonder how far one could really go.

For the moment, however, she only went back home.

Which wasn't very far by any standard, certainly not by her own, new one.

7

the fish
and the dead

So what now, you ask, fidgeting in your chair. Because you *are* fidgeting, aren't you. All this tea and chatter, where is it leading, is what you want to know.

Right now, it's going straight back to Layla's bed, where she lay, very quietly, wondering what it would take to be a real, clear-cut, no-doubt-about-it princess. One who would be admired from afar. One who'd command respect at first sight.

Wondering what it was she was missing, what could she spare.

What would she have to drop.

Whom.

Wondering, too, about love and cereal, looking at her husband, sleeping so heavily next to her. Measuring him up, you could say. Checking if he would do. How can he sleep so heavily, she thought, with that cold, sharp, hidden fury no one ever suspected her of hiding.

Now Layla knew a thing or two about princesses. She had read her fairy tales just like anyone else. And she knew this: you were either born one, or you became one. And you became one only by marrying a prince.

Only she was married already, wasn't she? And he was no prince, this was painfully clear by now. That glow she was after, it wouldn't be found at his side.

Now Layla had an aunt, her mother's aunt actually, who lived in a tiny hut by the beach. She was a merry woman, this aunt, who'd given up on all thought of hearth and home years and years ago, years before her niece's November wedding. No thought of love had ever troubled her heart. Indeed, she had come to serve the Winds so freely, she needed no mirrors at all to haunt her. Her long hair had been white for many a year now, and her brown skin was crinkly with years of sea-gazing.

This aunt spent her nights watching for drowning men and sinking ships, collecting the light they gave off just before going under. Bottles of light covered the shelves of her hut. One could see them glowing from afar. She'd bathe in light every morning, and bathe in light every evening, and she never cried a single tear. She ate fish, day in and day out, quick, silvery fish that she caught with her hands. Layla couldn't believe she had such an unbelievable aunt. Indeed, she almost forgot her every now and then, so unbelievable was she. But when she remembered, it always made her proud.

It now occurred to Layla that this aunt could be the answer to her problem. Because she was so simple-minded, you see. Because she knew so little of what she yet had to learn. So she thought, This aunt of mine, why, she's so special, she might just be a queen. And if—she thought, quite logically—I have a royal aunt, then I might be one after all. She was looking for proof, you see. Princess or no princess, that was the question. And a cold, empty castle, which could only be reached by scooter, didn't seem like much in the way of evidence.

So, one morning she went to visit her aunt. It was a two-hour drive by car, but Layla, she thought, This is the only way. If I'm to become a real princess, one that shows, it can't be by scooter. You see, at this point, she wanted to be quite an ordinary princess, one that walks about with a crown of sorts, for everyone to see. Such a childish Layla, really.

She found her aunt sitting by the sea-side, chanting. "Good morning, dear aunt," Layla said, which seemed to strike a pleasant, homely balance between humility and familiarity.

"Good morning Layla," said the aunt, just as always, unaware of her great-niece's concerns.

Now Layla, she had no time to spare. Remember how urgent all this had become. "Are you a Queen?" she asked her aunt very matter-of-factly.

"Of course I am," replied the aunt, and whoops, she caught a fish, and glump! in it went, head, slippery body, and tail.

This is too revolting, thought Layla.

How can she, she thought next.

Because she's royalty, she crossly answered herself. Royal personages may do as they please. They are often eccentric, she added, quoting from an old manual about royal demeanor, which she found years ago in her mother's attic and had lately been reading attentively.

So she sat there with her aunt, trying to catch fish, trying to pick up the chant:

Oh it's me and the fish,
Just me and the fish
Just me and the fish, just us.
Oh it's me and the dead,
Just me and the dead,
Just me and the dead after all.

She didn't like it. Not one bit. And those hands, those crinkly brown hands, they were smelly, weren't they? Was there no limit to this royal eccentricity she had read about? What had happened to obvious dignity? What about plain, fragrant beauty?

"Are you quite sure?" she asked the aunt, somewhat apprehensively.

"Of course I'm sure. I've told you time and again, haven't I?"

"You haven't told me anything, ever," insisted Layla.

"Not you. The others. Sooner or later you all come and ask me some such question. It was your turn now."

This was new. Quite new. So new she could hardly hear it. But it seemed to be true. Liora and Lenore had been there before her. "And mind you," added the aunt, "they were much quicker about it. Lenore came when she was twelve. And Liora was seventeen. I did wonder when you would show up. But then, you've always been slow. Didn't even have any tits till you were twenty, did you?" And she let out a hoarse laugh.

None of this was pleasant, you can be sure. How could it be? Here she was, later than everyone else, laughed at with that raspy laugh.

"I guess you'll run away now," said the aunt. "You're like Liora. One stinky fish and she was gone forever. Lenore did better. I taught her a trick or two. She even worked with me at night."

"With the dead?" Layla gasped. "When she was twelve?"

"With the dead. The thankless dead. She was very good at it, really, so I let her keep the bottles she filled."

"You didn't."

"Of course I did. Ever tried one of her perfumes?" And she laughed again, almost horribly. "But she didn't stay very long," the aunt said, sighing quite wistfully. "Said she preferred to work with the living. Said she would learn to steal men's hearts. Said they were a nasty lot, all of them. They wouldn't even feel it if their hearts were gone. Didn't deserve to have any in the first place. Asked me to give her some extra-sharp nails to work with. And I most certainly did. Agreed with every word of hers, that's why. Told her she'd be doing us all a favor. Tidying up, actually. You should be one to appreciate tidiness!" And she laughed yet again, visibly pleased with her great-niece's dismay.

At this point Layla felt she could be as rude as she pleased. After all, she too had learned a trick or two, in Alaska. "So how come you're so smelly if you're a Queen?" she asked. "How come you eat these disgusting fish and wear these ugly rags? How come no one's ever heard about you, if you're so bloody royal, huh?"

"Because," replied the aunt as she caught yet another shiny fish, "because that's the kind of Queen I am. The kind I choose to be. And if you don't like it, you can run back home to your dear husband and your scented closets and forget all about it. Spend your life having babies, like your mother. We've seen how much good that did her. But if you stay, I'll teach you a trick or two, too. Who knows? Maybe you're the one, maybe there's more to you than your mousy appearance reveals." And the aunt sighed, and swallowed her fish with quite a show of weary disappointment. "I did always hope one of you would stay. I'm old now, you know, much older than you think. I have this hut, and I have all these bottles, I'd hoped to leave them to someone when I'm gone. But Liora, she's too fussy, Lenore's too ambitious for this kind of work, and Lihi is way too simple."

"What about Luna?" Layla asked.

"Oh Luna, that fool, that goose, that pile of mush—she's too soft inside. Couldn't even make it as a regular live woman, she certainly can't be Queen of the Drowning Dead." She seemed quite bitter now, this fishy royal aunt. She sounded almost normal, the way she grumbled and put everyone down. Finally Layla had some sense of family

But she was quite annoyed about this last bit, you see. Luna had always been her most beloved sister. "I don't think you're a Queen at all," she said. "I think you're mad, if you want to know. It was very wrong of you to give Lenore those nails. It hasn't done her any good at all. And you're wrong about Liora, and Lihi, and Luna too. But mostly, you're wrong about me; I'm not mousy at all. As a matter of fact, I'm doing quite well, thank you. I have a flying scooter, and I have a castle that's all my own, a real castle, a clean and gorgeous castle. And I have my own personal elf-friend. And yes, I do have a husband, a fairly good one actually, and I have three lovely daughters, who have had the good fortune never ever to have met you. So you see, I don't need your fish and I don't need your dead and I very sincerely hope never to see you again!"

What a speech! What a stand to take! Makes you quite proud of her, doesn't it? Of course the speech wouldn't do at all if the aunt were a real Queen, but for once, Layla decided to risk it. And would you believe it, no sooner had she said the last nine words, along with a brisk shake of her bracelet, than—*whoosh!*—the aunt disappeared, just like that. No more smelly hands, no barky laughter, no filthy hut! It does make you wonder what else Layla could whoosh away. She certainly wondered a bit, too.

Back to the house she went. There's just no way she could whoosh that into oblivion, such a solid, weighty disturbance, closets-full of it, too cumbersome for any such whooshing.

Too comforting, at times.

There were her roses, in need of pruning, the curtains to be dusted, the girls to be hugged. Those soft cheeks and clear brows, all that "Oh Mommy," the look of wonder in their eyes whenever she said anything at all.

They're so lovely, she thought. So perfect, so fresh, so unsuspecting: my little ones, who'll never lay eyes on that weird aunt of mine, who'll never need to do what I've done, never need to know what I've known.

My sweets.

My perfect ones.

My little princesses.

So this was the time for laces and frills and endless bows. What a fuss of shopping and singing, what a stream of baking and playing, "Oh Mommy," "Oh Mommy," all over the place, it made her glow with pride.

There's more than one way to become a Queen, she thought with great satisfaction as she paraded the girls back and forth on her little street. There they were, on a Saturday afternoon, Layla and daughters and husband too, nice and clean, if only they had a carriage they'd be waving at you, rigid-wristed.

It was a peaceful time, and the husband, he was so pleased, he bought her a diamond necklace that showed off very nicely on her black velvet dress.

Not that she wore it very often.

You see, all that baking and playing, all that strolling and mending, it made her feel just a bit tired. She'd slip into any old dress she found, and she wasn't changing them very often, not with all those piles of laces and frills that filled the washer to the brim and over.

Just a bit tired, that's what she was.

Just a bit frazzled, with all that "Mommy come, Mommy give" her princely girls were getting so good at.

But she prodded herself, our Layla, relentlessly.

It takes hard work, she kept reminding herself, and at least I'm warm here, and my girls are so happy.

And yet, those soft cheeks were still wet with tears twice a day. Big, royal tears. And quite a lot of simple wailing. Nagging too, would you believe it? And screaming, just every now and then. There she was, washing the dishes, and her little girl just crying. "*Wa-wa-wa*" it went, princess or no princess. Layla almost wished she could whoosh her away, but she settled for some slapping instead. It was, after all, the more maternal thing to do.

She needed a break, that's what. But she wasn't taking one. Not the movies, not by herself. Not the beach, not anymore. When you think of it, she never went anywhere closer than Alaska if she couldn't get her husband to come along. Which she couldn't, that was very clear by now.

And so, after seven more weeks of patient waiting, seven dutiful weeks, seven weeks of searching for the treasures within, so to speak, Layla went on her next trip. Europe, she said to herself; somewhere mild and safe, somewhere civilized and tame. Why not?

"Take me to *Prague*," she quietly commanded, the *P* and the *G* softly melting in her mouth, the *A* just a bit longer than you'd expect.

The scooter was obedient as ever, and rose very gently into the air; and Layla, she just sat there, on that little space where you'd usually rest your foot, and enjoyed the view.

8

a whore
or a witch

Now there was one thing Layla hadn't quite reckoned with. People went on living even when she wasn't there, right? Others had their own scores to settle. Take the husband, for instance. Cooking lunch and then dinner for himself and those little girls, putting them to sleep, trying to remember Layla's lullabies. Clearing the dishes. Sitting all alone in front of the TV, waiting for his wife to come home. Wondering if she would stay away all night, wondering what would happen, where she would go next. Getting somewhat fed up with all of this. Feeling somewhat grouchy. After all, it's not every wife who has a flying scooter, who plays at mother one day, at princess the other, who gazes at you for hours every time you try to fall asleep. "Why can't she be normal?" he thought. Which very quickly led him to wonder if it could be true, could it be possible, that she has quite absolutely stopped being normal? And what would this mean, what would this mean for all of us?

Getting angry, that's what he was.

"Who knows where she goes with that scooter?" he thought next, "Who knows whom she meets?"

"Are you sure she isn't sleeping around?" his father had asked some time ago, after Layla's second trip to Alaska.

"All this talk about scooters," said the father, "In my day, one just had affairs. She's just making it up, boy. I mean, did you ever see her fly?"

"Certainly not," said the husband. "You could just as well ask me to hire a detective to follow her around."

"That wouldn't be such a bad idea," said his father. "You see, if she's just sleeping around and making all this up, she's a whore and a liar. And if she really believes she has a flying scooter, then she's crazy. But if the scooter can fly, why, that makes her a witch, doesn't it?" A short smile played around the father's lips. He was pleased with his rhetoric, especially pleased with this last little joke. But the smile disappeared as he drew in for the punch, "In any case, boy, get a divorce, and quick."

"But I love her," said the husband.

"I always knew she was different," he added, trying to be fair.

"What about the girls?" he asked next.

"Well, you managed quite well when she was in so-called bloody Alaska," replied the father, "and they're better off without a crazy whore for a mother." He really did care about his son, you see, and he had never had too much patience for his starry-eyed daughter-in-law. Nuts, that's what he called her, even before the scooter, for, unlike his son, he had seen a certain gleam in her eye from time to time, and he didn't like it. She'd be serving dinner and chatting very pleasantly, and his son would be sitting there, quietly admiring her, and then, suddenly, she'd say something strange. Once it was about fairies; another time she said she'd like to travel around the world with her family, like a gypsy. "I've seen children sleep with their parents at train stations," she had said. "I saw them in Venice, in their sleeping bags. I saw them in Greece, on the beach. Dirty. Snug. Happy. I wish we could do that some time."

The father would sit there, waiting for his son to say something.

Which he didn't.

What a fool he is, thought the father, letting her get away with all this nonsense.

But at least—he always summed up the situation—at least she can cook. And words, well, words can't really make that much of a difference.

This adultery, though, or else madness, was definitely not something he would tolerate. A nice, trim father he was, a no-nonsense kind of father, a truly respectable one. And if his son wouldn't, or couldn't see that he was behaving like a fool, he'd have to set him straight.

Only the son wasn't such a fool, not the kind who would do just as he was told. He didn't like this talk about whores, and he didn't like the idea of detectives, and he definitely didn't like being bossed around. Madness, on the other hand, was not something to be trifled with. Not an issue you could just ignore. Not with all those little girls in the house.

Sitting there, all alone now, without any kind of comfort, it did seem to him that a wife with a flying scooter, who scooted away to Alaska and Prague (she had told him this time, as if she were giving the baby-sitter her phone number in case of emergency)—well a wife like this wasn't wasn't really the normal thing to have. He was getting cross, remember. Because even if he didn't talk to Layla, even if he didn't go in for all that searching and wondering she had submitted him to lately, he did like to hear her walking around the house. Those quick steps of hers, that slamming of closets and drawers, the occasional bump into a wall. Even the broken dishes, one or two a week, just because her movements were so restless and dry.

So he started wondering what he should do.

Something, he realized, had to be done.

Why, next thing she'd start taking the girls. Who knows? She might just stay there some day.

Even if she didn't leave forever, even if she kept coming back in time to make lunch, the husband felt it was time for initiative. Something that would make Layla sit still; and listen; and simmer down; perhaps something that would make her hurt.

Just a little.

Just a bit.

Because he found himself, all of a sudden, thoroughly annoyed. Harassed, really. Seven years of this, seven weeks of that, someone must put a stop to all of this, he thought.

Now you mustn't think he was slow-witted. Not a bit

of it. Quiet, that's what he was. And slow to move. But he was thorough, thorough in his thinking, thorough in his welling rage.

It now occurred to him that he needed an ally in all of this, someone to confide in, to consult with. And it would have to be done properly, decently. It would be too easy to cast him as the bastard, he knew that. Because he knew how far Layla had longed to go, how twisted the passages had become with time. She had complained, hadn't she? Bitterly. She had begged. So often. And he had just sat there, waiting for it to end. Hoping it would go away. He couldn't really pretend to be surprised.

So whatever he did now, it would have to be done right.

Because he wanted to seem fair.

Because more than that, even, he truly wanted to feel fair.

So after sitting there in the living room for a few hours, very still, very red in the face, very white around the nostrils, he decided on his move. He'd talk to Layla's sisters, express his concern. Ask for their opinion, maybe learn something new. Get some advice. It was the right thing to do. Talk to them about their nieces, moaning in their sleep in the next room. They should care. It was important that they knew he cared. Genuinely. He wouldn't say anything about whores or witches, and the question of madness, why, that could be brought up gradually. Perhaps there wouldn't be any need. Maybe they would mention it first.

He got up and went to the phone. He didn't need the phone book. Always had a good memory for numbers.

Only he couldn't decide whom to call, whether to talk to all of them, in what order.

Lihi is too young, he thought. She probably thinks it's all so cool. She's insignificant, really. Lenore is too flashy, too cold. What could she know about marriage or children?

Liora. She was the natural choice. The eldest. The most sedate. Reasonable, that's what he always thought of her. Just a bit eccentric, with those white robes, but a true matron. A responsible mother of six. A good wife, that he knew for sure. He had often heard his brother-in-law talk about her devoted care, her constant attention, her quiet body in bed. He had even been jealous, at times.

Liora could be trusted. He would call her first.

Her quiet voice when she greeted him was immediately soothing. What a woman, he thought. And he asked her, casually as it were, "You know Layla has gone to Prague, don't you?"

Now Liora, she was no fool either. The husband had forgotten that. She knew very well, there hadn't been such a phone call, ever. *He* calling *her*? To chat about his wife? And who was he, anyway, to tell her things about her sister, as if she didn't know? (She didn't, actually. The transplant-party had ended somewhat sourly, remember?)

So she said, very coolly, "Uhum." She wasn't in any hurry, was she?

"Well, yes. Just this evening. She didn't even tuck in the girls," he blurted, and she could hear his angry blush over the phone.

This wasn't working as planned, not at all. He knew

it wasn't. Concern, that had been his idea. Upright, matter-of-fact concern. A dignified talk between two responsible grown-ups with a childish mother of three on their hands, one who insisted on flying around on a scooter as if there weren't any planes anymore, as if she couldn't just take a regular vacation like everyone else.

"I'm sure they're quite all right," said Liora. "But of course, if you need any help, I'll come right over."

So he thanked her and said that was very relieving and so on, made quite a mumbling fool of himself, just to cover up his traces.

And Liora, she hung up and thought, Little sister is walking a thin line. Soon she'll take one trip too many. But he won't get any help from me.

Because you see, even if Liora didn't like all this flying around, and even if she would prefer for Layla to calm down just a bit, she never, ever, let any man in on her plans.

Which isn't to say she didn't have any.

So much for Liora, thought the husband, and he called Lenore. Because he still felt that he had to do something, and he couldn't think of anything better to do.

Now Lenore wasn't impressed when she heard that Layla hadn't tucked in her girls. Good for her, she thought. She really has found someone, good for her.

But Lenore, she liked an intrigue. It amused her to hear the husband's pointed breathing on the phone. You see, she knew very well what he wanted. He's getting angry, she thought. How interesting. She had never seen him angry before, didn't even know he had it in him. And calling her, why, that was even more interesting. Besides, she'd always liked angry men. So she told him to come over the next day.

And had he been able to watch her over the phone, he would have seen a treacherous blue in her eye.

A child cried out from her room.

9

all those
little animals

Wasn't it lovely! Gorgeous! The cathedral just beneath her, sunny roads winding about, such freshness in the air, such crispness in every outline. Wonderful, wonderful Prague! Would she start with a café, with a stroll in a park? Would she talk to strangers? Oh she would, she would, she definitely would. Again and again, all at once, if only possible.

The scooter, however, landed just by the belfry. An odd little scooter it was, with whims of its own. A sense for the dramatic, perhaps. Or else a pious streak. Perhaps a taste for discipline.

"Good evening, dear Layla," said the bat. "I've been expecting you."

"Good evening," replied Layla, always polite.

"I'm here to help you," said the bat. "You seem so confused. Lost, I'd say. Why don't you tell me what's troubling you, Layla? I'm here to listen. Just relax and tell me what it is."

Now Layla, did she go in for all of this? Indeed she didn't. "I'll walk around just a bit, thank you," she said to the bat. "I've brought a map, actually, so it's quite all right. I'm a seasoned traveller, really."

Down she went, step after step, quickly. She had become quite wary of little animals, remember? Down she rushed, careful but light, light-footed, light-hearted Layla, ready for Prague, for adventure, ready for life, any life, so she thought. Down, down the steps, so many of them, worn, shiny, stony steps, caved in just the tiniest bit with the mark of thousands of hopeful, seasoned travellers, thousands of husbands and sisters, a thousand and one Laylas. Down, down the polished stairs, winding down, her heart anxious with joy, ready, oh so ready, ready for anything really. Clean autumn streets stretched ahead of her, and the square—of course there was a square—and clusters of people sitting about, clusters of pigeons, of souvenir stands, little groups of white-haired tourists, long-haired tourists, tourists of all sorts, and Layla, all alone, in their midst.

The first thing she noticed was the silence humming right between her ears. She didn't make much of it. So it's quiet here, she thought, that's quite nice actually. I wouldn't want it to be loud, not on such a lovely autumn day.

Which, as was so often the case with Layla, was only partly true. Even Layla, our black-and-white, all-or-nothing Layla, even she knew there could be just a few shades between noise and this irksome, bewildering silence. But

Layla was so ready, so willing, so very anxious for a perfect day, she couldn't afford to complain.

Not even silently.

Not even to herself.

So on she went, clutching her bag just a bit tighter. She didn't even notice how white her knuckles had become. The silence pounded in her head. She could feel that queasy silence in her throat, but she went on, our brave Layla. She really had become almost brave after all those patient weeks at home. I'll have a coffee, she thought; no, I'll have a beer; no, a glass of wine, that's what I'll have on my first day in Prague. They were really there, all those little cafés she'd imagined for years, the round little tables covered with white cloths, the shiny brass doorknobs, all there, just as they should be, nothing amiss, surely nothing to complain about. She sat at one of those tables and remembered not to let go of her bag: seasoned traveller that she was, she knew you shouldn't lose sight of your bag, not when you're all alone in a foreign city.

"A glass of wine, please," she said to the waiter, who was wiping off the clean table. It was such a quiet place, she could feel her voice rumbling through the vacant air.

"A glass of wine, please," she said again when he didn't answer. He didn't even look at her, never raised his eyes, never even stopped his wiping, as if no one had spoken.

Layla knew she could be just a bit timid, just a bit too quiet at times, and she certainly had to admit she was feeling more than a bit timid right now. So she raised her voice, and said quite sharply, so sharply it startled her, "Wine, please."

He didn't hear her. That was quite clear by now. Not a twitch of an ear, not a hint of a pause in his movements. He just swam around in that greasy silence that seemed to smother the city. "Please," she said again, quite ready to cry as he walked away, "please." But the word just bounced about in the still air, like a stray balloon once the party is over.

She got up. There really wasn't anything else she could do. She just got up and decided to try the next place.

It's not my fault he was so rude, she said to herself.

Maybe that's the way they are here, she thought. No one has ever told me a single thing about waiters in Prague.

And she reminded herself of the quick, impatient, dainty-footed garçons of Paris, Maybe they're like that here, she comforted herself, though she did have to admit there hadn't been anyone else in that café, and the waiter had seemed in no hurry at all.

So she did it again, all over, sat herself down at the next table, at the next wine-bar, and talked to the next waiter, asked him for that same glass of wine, which had already lost so much of its charm.

Yes, dearest, you've guessed so well. This waiter didn't answer either, and he didn't stop his wiping, not even for a fraction of a muscle. He walked away unhurriedly, just like the other one.

Did Layla get up as quickly?

Did she just look for the way to the next bar?

She did. She really, unbelievably did, even though her eyes were darting about, so worried, even though her mouth was soft with stifled sobs, her lips all blurred against the tender, pink skin around them.

And there's no need for guessing anymore. Of course, no one answered this time either.

She still had one try in her, though, so she said to herself, Forget the waiters, I'll try talking to someone else, and she approached the first person she saw, smoothing out her frightened hair, and asked for the way to the train station. Just for lack of a better question, really; the cathedral, after all, was right behind her, and the museums were obviously many. So a train station seemed a perfectly simple thing to ask for.

But even now no reply came, none at all.

She wouldn't cry. She couldn't risk a single tear, she knew that very well. If she started crying, why, there would be no end to it, and how would she manage a tour of the city with tears in her eyes? Going home, on the other hand, going back to her musty, cozy room, under the warm down quilt, deep, deep under—that was so easy. The scooter, after all, was patiently waiting for her. It would take her back in no time at all. But the smell of defeat, it was so overwhelming, it pulsated in her nose, in her stomach, she could feel it enveloping her like a vicious, slimy film.

I'm staying here, Layla said to herself. I'm staying here till this is over. Surely, whatever it is that's happening, it will stop after a while.

She walked about, trying to look at the shops and the houses, trying to do this as slowly as possible. She was sensible, our Layla, and since she was waiting for something to happen, it seemed reasonable to try and kill time as efficiently as possible. So she looked at the shop windows and tried to pay attention to every detail, compared prices of shoes she'd never even dream of buying, made mental notes of blue crystal vases hidden in dusty little shops, and all that while described Prague to anyone who would listen, summing it up, as it were, minute by minute, for future reference.

Only she kept glancing at her watch, and it had no good news for her. Slow as she tried to be, every shop took just a minute or two. Even when she tried keeping her eyes off those slow hands as long as possible, five minutes was all she could manage, and you really can't kill time with such small doses of indifference.

Yet she walked on.

After all, she had set herself a task.

Now, another thing Layla noticed was, she never seemed to get the cathedral out of her sight. She had turned right and left and followed every winding alley, and still she ended up back at the square, the vast mass of stone lumbering above her. Once, twice, five times she found herself under its cold shadow, no matter how often she looked at the map, which seemed to offer at least seven ways of leaving the place and finally seeing Prague. All of it.

It's that bat! she finally realized, It's that horrible, smelly bat! I should have known from the start!

And she rushed up the stairs, up, up, quick as a summer storm, as an evening fury, quick as shattered illusions, up, up, all the way back to the belfry.

"Stop it right now!" she snapped at the sleepy creature, or was he just pretending?

"What, dearest Layla, what should I stop?" he asked.

"You've been trying to ruin this trip for me. You've made them all deaf, stop it!" she said, and the tears finally frothed at her eyes.

"You don't really think I could make them all deaf, Layla. How could I? You overrate me. Perhaps it's your voice, dearest, maybe you were just too shy to speak up. It's been known to happen, and especially to you." Which was true, she knew it was true, it had happened so many times before, at home, on the street, and not only in the morning, when she had forgotten the sound of her voice, not only then, but late afternoons too, when the evening stretched so long ahead of her, and even on sunny, simple days, when she wasn't sure what it was she could say.

"You're doing it. I know you are. You're all alike. But I'm not giving up, not this time," and she stamped her foot.

"That works for the mink, my dear," the bat said in a mellow, gray voice. "The mink has always been quite alarmed at the least show of anger. But that, I'm glad to say, is a weakness I don't have. It's perfectly natural for you to be angry, dear, it really is, and it's quite all right with me. Go ahead, you can stamp your other foot, if it makes you feel better. You can also shout—come on Layla, it will do you good. I can see how angry you are."

"Oh shut up, shut up, you're just like him," she said, "I know you are. Next thing you'll do, you'll say there's nothing to see here. You'll send me home. I know you will."

"Well, that wouldn't be such a bad idea, really," said

the bat, and gently nestled in Layla's hair. "But you're wrong about me. I'd never dream of telling you what to do. That's for you to decide, dear Layla. And I certainly wouldn't tell you there's nothing to see. How could I? You've seen for yourself how lovely it all is."

"It is, it really is," Layla said, wistfully fingering her hair, touching the bat from time to time, surprised to discover how smooth his wings felt, surprised no less at the thought she was touching a bat, wondering where this could lead. It wouldn't be something to tell anyone about, that's for sure.

"You see, I'm not trying to pull any tricks," said the bat, but I wouldn't quite believe him if I were you. Or Layla. "No tricks, dear. But we do have to talk about what happened down there. They never heard you, did they? And you really couldn't seem to find your way ahead. Now how do you explain that? Poor orientation, perhaps? I'm concerned, Layla, you seemed to have quite a problem down there, and it's time we talked about it."

Was she tempted by his mildness? Did she really want to listen? The bat didn't pause to settle these questions. "You see, Layla, I know how timid you are. And I'm not all that sure you should be here, all by yourself. You could come here with your family. Prague is truly wonderful in the spring. You could come with your sisters, that would also be quite all right. But this scooter, dear, well, it worries me. More than a bit. I don't know if you've really thought out all the implications." The bat flew out from Layla's hair, which was now in a nervous tangle. It was flying above her head, in little circles, but she wasn't looking. She just sat there, sucking a strand of hair.

"I may have done something about your voice," he finally confessed.

She wasn't responding, you see. He felt he had to make a concession or two. It wouldn't do for Layla to just sit there crossly, ignoring his studied, mellow tones. He had to engage her in active conversation if anything were to be achieved. "It was for your own good, Layla," he insisted. "It's just a bit too risky, that's what I'm trying to say. I don't like it. I'm not sure you like it. I'm not sure you should. You are a mother of three, after all."

Ding!—that's all she said for an answer. She didn't even say it, just shook her bracelet, with a tired jerk of her hand. She'd heard enough of this. She could feel every word of his sinking all the way down to her feet, making them heavier by the minute.

Ding! Ding! Ding! echoed the tower, and the bat vanished, as easy as shaking off dust.

Layla took out the African comb from her bag, and sat down to fix her hair, very calmly. "We'll see now," she said, and her voice was as firm as a mother's when she's finally made up her mind. "We'll see what the waiter does now. We'll see how Prague unfolds for me now. I'm sure those alleys will start leading somewhere."

Once her hair was smoothed out she tied it up in a ribbon and walked down the stairs, as if no bat had ever troubled her.

It did seem different now. The movements weren't so slow anymore. She could finally hear the wind rattling through the trees, a musician tuning her harp, a guide droning on about the wonders of Prague. This is it, she told herself. This is what I expected, this mild bustle, and everyone looking so happy, so interested. All the faces seemed to have that in common: everyone seemed to be there with no other thought in mind but pleasure. Even the guide had put on a friendly grimace, and his audience, well, all of them were paying close attention, and if they weren't, they pretended. Everyone was looking just as they should, everything was in it rightful place, and Layla, all alone, was walking about, glancing at the souvenirs, going about the business of pleasure in a very calm way. She even stopped for a hot dog, asked for it in a voice so loud it earned her a few stares. But she just kept asking, asking for some mustard, then for some coke, checking her voice, balancing it till it came out just fine. After she finished her hot dog, carefully chewing each bite for as long as possible, she slowly threw away the paper cup and the napkin and walked on.

I'm in no hurry now, she occasionally told herself, no hurry at all. I could go to a museum, for instance, or have an ice cream. I'm here to please myself, that's what. So she walked on, and this time the streets led her just as they should. They were friendly, these streets, they always had something nice for her just around the corner, and for a while Layla forgot her watch and forgot her scooter, she even forgot the task of enjoying herself. She just followed the alleys, as they came, never even glancing at her map, just walking along, without even bothering to hum a tune, which was another thing she often did to do away with a stretch of time.

She just walked on and on, truly curious.

It was in one of these alleys that she saw the medicine chest. Or perhaps it was a bathroom cabinet, it wasn't easy to tell. But it was shiny, it sparkled, it was actually plated with mirror, three mirrored doors, and mirrors on the sides, bright as a summer-jewel. Someone just threw it out, Layla thought. Someone decided not to have so many mirrors in his bathroom anymore. Maybe mirrors troubled him in the mornings, Layla thought. This someone had also decided to throw out an old sofa. It stood there, right in the middle of a tiny square, with the shiny cabinet on top of it. The brown leaves still clinging to the trees and the scraps of gray-blue sky visible among them glistened in those three silvery doors, and you couldn't really tell, even had you been there, if they were the same leaves, over and over again, shining once in every door, three brown jewels for every withered leaf.

This is truly enchanted, thought Layla.

This must be magic, she thought.

Surely if I look into this mirror something will be revealed.

It was only her face, though, and there was nothing enchanting about it. Three pursed mouths, six pale, yellowish cheeks, three hints of trouble between the eyebrows, which gave so much away.

"This won't do," Layla said to herself, "I look so cross, so sad, so strict, school-teacher strict, bloody-nun strict; bitter-strict. How can I? Why do I look like that? It isn't right, it most certainly won't do, and why on earth did I tie up my hair? I look like a nervous mouse, I really do. I wish I could look just a bit nicer."

"It's all right," said the elf. "It's all right, you don't even have to let down your hair, Layla. You're fine."

He was wearing white again, somewhat soiled, somewhat gray, just enough to blend in with the buildings around them.

"There's a pattern to this," said Layla, a truly happy smile finally shimmering on her face.

"There certainly is," said the elf. "You see, Layla, everything is all right, there's nothing to worry or fear about, everything will be quite all right."

Now you may have heard this or that about elves. Their reputation is quite ambiguous, it's true. But this was a truly good-natured elf, without a single evil thought on his mind, no pranks at all, just benign concern for the first Layla he had happened to meet. Light-hearted, that's what he was, always on the lookout for a bright snatch of hopefulness. A silly elf, you might well say, quite ignorant of the ways of the world. Irresponsible, you might think, especially when promising so much. But he was well-intentioned, and surely that counts.

It certainly did for Layla.

"You're quite sure, are you?" she said, and had you been there, her eager, ready trust might have broken your heart.

And the elf nodded, with the smallest of elfish nods.

"So what happens now?" Layla asked. Someone, after all, would be in charge of this day.

"What happens now?" she promptly repeated, with just a trace of impatience.

"Whatever you like," said the elf. He really didn't

mean to tease her, even if that's what she thought. He was just being himself, going about his job, as it were. He was a wish-granting elf, remember. No less, but certainly no more.

"I don't know what I want," Layla replied.

Here they were, standing in the middle of the street. She could see the elf's reflection in all three mirrors. He looked so kind, so attentive, quietly standing there, waiting for her to make a wish, any wish at all.

"I don't understand this," Layla confessed. "You and the scooter. What is this all about, how did you happen, and to me, of all people?"

"I don't know about you," the elf replied, quite truthfully. "As for me, Layla, well, consider me your own personal bit of luck. A shiny coin you've found on the street, a lottery ticket you've kept and forgotten, and has finally brought in the prize. I'm your elf-friend, Layla, your very own. And you are my personal princess, the princess whose every wish is my command."

"But what kind of a princess am I?" Layla petulantly asked. "A dazzling, daring, dashing princess? A courageous, calm, confident one? Bold and brave? Bitter and bashful? Boring, perhaps?"

"You'll run out of letters, Layla," the elf wisely warned her.

"So what kind?" Layla asked again, her voice raised, no timidity in it at all, not now, when she knew just whom to be cross with.

"A flying princess, for all I can tell," said the elf. "I thought you had said so yourself."

"That was a joke," said Layla, who hadn't read enough about elves after all, and didn't know they were absolutely devoid of humor. "That was just something to say to the mink, to make him shut up. Who's ever heard of a flying princess?"

"You could always be the first," the elf politely proposed.

Getting on her nerves, that's what he was. "What are you being so cheerful about?" she asked him, almost viciously. "Can't you see this won't do? It's like that castle you gave me last time. I really didn't know what to do with it." She was calming down just a bit now, but, as was always the case with Layla, this was only a step on the way between anger and sobbing, with hardly any time for a pause in between.

"It was so empty," she cried, not crying, really, just letting her eyes fill over with tears, which she caught with the dry back of her hand just before they slid off her cheek. "It was so cold, and dark, and empty, why did you give me such an empty castle? I could hear the Winds rushing along every corridor, echoing in every hall. Why did it have to be so empty? It's just like me to get such an empty castle, and such a stupid, stupid elf!"

Will she be punished? You're worried now, aren't you? Perhaps a bit cross, cross with Layla, actually, who was being so rude; perhaps you even think she should be punished. She wasn't being very nice, really, was she? Not at all grateful, or gracious, or whatever.

"Will she be punished? Will she have to pay for this?" you ask.

No, dearest. This elf had no punishing in him, none

at all. He was just the perfect kind of elf you'd want to have for yourself, perfect as a sunset with champagne, perfect as four scoops of ice cream with chocolate topping, perfect as your dearest wish come true. He never even answered her. He was in no hurry, you see, and had no other mission at all, just to stand there and wait for Layla to make her wish, or at least to try and trace a tail of a wish, if only possible.

Which he did, right then.

"It was empty," he admitted. "That might have been a mistake. But that's easy to fix, Layla, really. See how easily I fix it, just look and see!"

And surely, as she watched, the castle grew all around her, and there she was, in the very center of the most splendrous hall ever, and the armchairs and vases and flowers, they were multiplying by the second. The elf was doing a terrific job, he really was, all the way down to the curtains—brocade and damask, satin and muslin, anything you, or Layla, could possibly wish for—and he didn't stop at that, no indeed. This time the elf was trying to give each word of Layla's the widest possible interpretation, and even if this was usually a difficult thing for him to do—his training having been in precision, generally, in the strict fulfillment of dreams, no personal initiatives, thank you— elves, too, can learn new ways, and he really was trying to do his best for Layla.

So now an orchestra sprang up in front of her, and yes! yes! there were guests, too, many of them, they all stood there, waiting for her to give the sign. Their eyes offered everything any Layla could wish for—expectation, admiration—there's nothing strict about your mouth, said their eyes. Even your hair is just fine, said their eyes. Everything about you is right, Layla, you're our princess, our queen. Come and join in the dance. You'll know all the steps this time, you'll be graceful, Layla, you'll be tall and nimble, you'll be beautiful, Layla, you don't even need to let down your hair.

Oh she danced and danced and danced. She whirled all over the ballroom, she shone in a thousand and one mirrors, never even pausing to check her reflection, changing partners without a thought, with no clock to time her, no stroke of twelve to worry about, and no . . . no Prince to flee from.

10
just give me
the answer, please

The house was so empty.

He didn't like it, not one bit.

Layla is taking her time on this trip, he thought, She said she'd be back before the girls woke up. He could remember how punctual she always was, punctual to the point of nuisance, constantly glancing at the kitchen watch, sticking to her schedule, planning the precise number of minutes for every step of her day. Even when she had first found her scooter he could remember her rushing into the house just on time to make lunch, shaking off the snow from her hair, breathlessly on time, always.

But now the minutes were so long and heavy, and she was gone.

It was strange really, how uncomfortable he felt. Hadn't he always asked for some quiet? Hadn't he always told Layla to go off and do whatever she pleased, but please, please to leave him alone?

Of course he had, time and again.

So did he remember all this, now that he was so cross? Did he ask himself, Why did I let her fly off to Prague? Should I have taken her somewhere myself? Maybe he did, maybe he didn't. He wasn't one to ask too many questions; answers were more in his line. And that was precisely what he was after now. Some clear, solid answers.

So he stacked up the breakfast dishes and he put the bread back in the box, and then he put on a clean shirt. He was neat in his ways, this husband of Layla's, quite capable around the house when he wanted to, really. There's no doubt he could manage very well by himself if he ever had to, which he somewhat fleetingly pointed out to himself right then. I could manage very well by myself if she ever left, this thought hummed itself in his mind as he put back a few toys in their places, not Layla's places, perhaps, but perfectly reasonable ones in their own right. It's strange, he thought, Layla always seems so busy. I know she's busy, yet here I am without her, and there doesn't seem to be that much to do.

This point we shall not discuss right now, dearest. We can't, really. Such a messy, difficult point, and not at all necessary right now, with so many other points giving us quite a hard time, thank you.

Let us stick to the husband for a while, watch him walk around the house with measured steps, never bumping into anything, of course not. Perhaps, he's even hearing some morning music. He's in no dreadful hurry, he rarely is. It's this calm neatness of his, this way he has of folding back a newspaper, of putting the right lid on every tin of coffee or sugar, that's always made Layla admire him. While at the same time, of course, it's made her despise him to no small extent.

She had never known someone as profoundly neat as he, his socks sorted by color, his books by size, his few passions sorted by order of satisfaction obtainable. And when he did the dishes, during those short weeks before she decided she could marry him—why not?—when he did the dishes, he always stacked them in ways so neat she had to admit he outdid her. Absolutely. He had learned so many useful things from his mother, he really had. He could do all kinds of surprising things, like glaze a cake and dress a chicken and toast bread to golden perfection. He didn't even make a mess in the kitchen, which was more than one could ask of any man, right?

Now those measured steps of his, those quiet, regulated movements, there was a cramped impatience about them. And a trace—you'd have to live with him for seven years to notice, but a definite trace—of discomfort.

Unease, one might say.

A bad conscience, perhaps?

A tie won't be necessary, he decided, but he did put on a jacket, and he looked at himself in the mirror for just a hint of a minute longer than usual. "It must be done," he said to himself, never noticing how those branches were swaying by the window, never noticing how set his jaw had become.

He would be meeting Lenore in half an hour, nine-thirty, she had said. He was quite surprised that she appointed him such an early hour; he had always thought of Lenore as someone who woke up just before noon. "Are you sure that's convenient," he had asked her on the phone, and she just said, "Oh, quite convenient," but even then her voice sounded full of unpleasant smiles.

Now the husband wasn't really glad to meet Lenore, just remember how shiny and black her clothes always were—quite unsettling in a sister-in-law. And that chilly, smooth blond hair, how could one square that off with family ties? Lenore was really more than he wished to handle, only now he seemed to have no choice. He needed some answers. He needed to know. He needed to plan ahead, either way. But he wouldn't let it get complicated, he wouldn't let her make fun of him in that detached, barely perceptible way of hers, he wouldn't get into any long talks about Layla or life. This would be the first time he ever visited Lenore by himself, but he wouldn't let the newness of it get in the way of his purpose. And his purpose was clear enough, he didn't have to ponder about it. It was his special talent to know such things without any thought at all, like someone tying shoelaces in the dark, his fingers deft through years of habit.

An answer, that's all he needed. He wasn't talking to his father now, he wasn't trying to make excuses for Layla. Surely the time for excuses had passed. That long cold night had made his purpose quite clear for him: he wanted it all to stop. Either way. He didn't want a flying wife, he didn't want a flying mother for his little girls. So he needed to know.

He didn't even need to think of questions to ask, he only wanted one answer, and he hoped Lenore would have it ready for him:

What was Layla going to do next.

He just needed that one answer, you see. He was fed-up with waiting, he wanted to know. Either way. Because it did occur to him, in occasional moments between impatience and indifference, that all kinds of trouble might lie ahead. He knew his wife very well, after all, like all husbands. (They do, dearest, they really do, no matter how oblivious they choose to be.) He did know precisely what it was that Layla hungered for, even if he pretended not to. And he knew, he knew very well, that he couldn't offer it.

He wouldn't.

So now he just needed to know, that's all.

Would she or wouldn't she?

Leave.

Settle down.

Anything definite.

He slammed the door. A quick, short slam this door had never experienced till then. This door had always been treated gently. It had been carefully locked both inside and out, whenever the husband left the house, whenever he did his nightly rounds before he pronounced the day over. Layla had left it open most of the time. Even if she left the house to go somewhere nearby, she preferred to take the risk. Empty hands, that's what our Layla liked to feel. No metallic jumble of keys for her itchy fingers, nothing to hold, nothing to drop—she seemed to drop things so easily lately. And when she came back home, well, she never quite closed the door, it seemed nicer to forego that dry, unfriendly click. To have the house just a bit open. Just a bit.

But now the door was slammed, and the car door, it was slammed, too, in a measured kind of way, just enough to communicate frustration, if anyone were watching, but never betraying his rage. His stayed, pickled anger.

What would Layla do next?

Would she come back and walk through the door with that ask-me-no-questions face, so irritating and yet relieving?

Could she be made to leave that bloody scooter alone?

He really couldn't let her go on flying like this, that was clear by now. His own father was mocking him, for God's sake, and so were the sisters. In no time at all the neighbors would catch on.

What would Layla do next? Could she really just stay there, in Prague, or wherever it was that her fancy had taken her? Could she just walk away from the cozy, snug life he had cherished for seven years? And what about the girls? He did care about the girls, you see. They were his very own, he had bathed and fed them with meticulous care, always. Or often, at least. What would happen to them?

But these are just a few of the questions, you might say.

And you'd be right, dearest, every single one of these questions could be splintered off into many more: What about the house, the car? Who would take the books? How would they divide the time, or the girls? How would they split up their little lives? What about love? Did he still—it would be easy for you to think up more and more questions. Out of sympathy with his plight, perhaps; out of experience, who knows?

But the husband, I've said, wasn't in the mood for such questions.

Would she or wouldn't she? That's all he really wanted to know.

And in case it occurs to you that he could also think up a whole other kind of question, why, then it's simplicity itself that's guiding you. If you're thinking he could ask Lenore for help, he could try and do something to make Layla happy, maybe he should join her on one of her trips—if indeed you're thinking all of that, well, what can I say? You break my heart, you really do.

Because he could do all of this. Three sisters-in-law, three women to turn to for help, three innocent girls with no idea of life's trickery, yes, of course he could ask other questions. Only he wouldn't. And it wasn't because he was evil, and it wasn't because he didn't care. I've said this already, yet I repeat it, imagining your critical frown: you don't like this husband right now. Maybe you mistrust all story-book husbands, maybe its husbands in general you disapprove of. But this husband, this shoelace-in-the-dark husband of Layla's, well, if you only chose to, you could actually feel for him. He hadn't really done anything to deserve all of this, that's what he thought at every red light on the way, and even if he was so silent, one could argue his point very well for him: seven years of quiet loyalty, seven years of quiet firmness, seven long years of quiet love, even.

Love of the kind Layla didn't want, that's for sure, love of the kind you wouldn't settle for, perhaps, but the very best love he had to give.

All of it.

Unswerving.

Unquestioning, as has already been pointed out.

Much more than could ever be said for Layla.

And there was another thing that guided the husband's silent, focused, furious driving: with deft, unknowing knowledge, he had chosen to seek only those answers he could swallow. For there was one thing this husband was absolutely certain about: he may not have known about dusty roads, and he may not have known about distant horizons, but he knew his own limitations. Sometimes he was fond of them and sometimes he wasn't, but he always treated them with utmost respect. So the question of making her stay, the question of what he could do to make her stay, stay for good, this question was no part of his shoelacing. He had done all that he could, he had been all that he would, and if that wouldn't do, then sad as it made him feel, there was nothing he could add.

Indeed he was sad. He did have a preferred outcome, even if he didn't do a thing to make it come about. But he drove on, silent as ever, and if he had a thought now and then it was an angry one, mostly about Layla, who had made things so difficult, but also about Lenore, who would probably make them worse, who would certainly make the most of this opportunity.

Him coming to ask her for something, she'd certainly enjoy that.

Lenore, meanwhile, was getting ready. Not in any special kind of way, just her usual, slow, morning readiness. Coffee, a quick look at the newspaper. A long shower with her special soap, which made every trace of nightmare vanish from her body, careful use of the right creams and lotions, all bottled up and neatly labeled: Quiet Glamour and Confidence cream, Quick Retention and Reply lotion—Lenore always knew how to make an efficient cosmetic preparation, and she certainly knew when and how to use it. Right now she added her Morning Innocence mascara, and just a blush of Friendly Face rouge. She brushed out her hair vigorously, as her mother had taught her, and she used a bow to keep it away from her forehead, which she had treated with her old Anti-Wrinkles/No Trouble cream. Almost an hour passed before she emerged from her bathroom, naked in spite of the morning chill. She wrapped her body in a clean white sheet, and dreamily walked about her apartment, smiling her little, secret smiles, smiles none of her sisters had ever seen. Smiles intended for men only.

Dressing didn't require a very long time. Her clothes were all quite similar. She kept them that way for simplicity's sake, clothes having never mattered much to Lenore, as long as they were new and trim and preferably black. Black trousers, black shirt, black sneakers, black socks. As far as socks were concerned, she always bought the very same kind. She didn't like troubling herself with finding pairs, she just threw all her black, identical socks in one big drawer, and took pride in saving the time her sisters wasted on such trite affairs.

She was ready now. She even had time for another coffee. It was only nine o'clock.

Lenore didn't really like getting up so early, noon was always a better time for her, but she knew everything one needed to know about throwing people off their balance. It was a trick she had had ever since childhood: think what mother, or your teacher, or anyone, really, expects you to do—and don't do it. Or do the opposite. The comfort of habit seemed such a petty one compared to the benefits one could reap this way: the look of surprise, the split-second of indecision, the hesitation she could sense and use to her advantage.

"Lenore is full of surprises . . ."

"You always need to stay on your toes when Lenore's around . . ."

"Lenore will catch you off guard when you're least ready . . ."

Those old, familiar sentences were waltzing about in her mind. They fed some of those little smiles of hers while she sipped her coffee.

She could imagine her brother-in-law getting ready for their appointment, taking trouble to look even neater than usual, trying to look casual at the same time, making sure he would be punctual, trying not to be too punctual at the same time. Lenore could easily imagine all of this: those little moments of hesitation she created in others had given her so much time to observe them. People were easy to figure out, Lenore thought. It always amused her that they didn't know this, that they took such trouble to try and pretend.

Now Lenore, she had no such problems. She had all her special vanishing creams, some her very own gift and others she had worked hard to get—worked with the living and worked with the dead, just as her aunt had taught her. She knew how to capture the light that poured out of a man's adoring heart, knew how to use it. She had her special tubes and jars, all marked with dates of production and expiration.

So she sat there and waited for him. She always preferred to be ready ahead of time and had woken up at seven to make time for deliberate slowness, for ease, to make time for extra time. No one had ever seen Lenore out of breath, and this husband of Layla's, he certainly wouldn't be the first.

Did Lenore make any plans for her meeting?

Did she wonder what he wanted of her?

No, to both questions.

Lenore knew very well what he wanted of her, and she never, ever, made plans for a meeting. She just made sure she was perfectly ready for it. As far as this husband was concerned, he was so simple. Transparent really. Lenore knew what he wanted, even if she phrased it in words quite different than his.

Approval, that's what.

He expects my approval, she thought, and no cream could hide the contempt twisted in her mouth. He wants me to say that everything he's done is fine. He wants me to say everything he might do next is fine, too. But he won't say any of this. I wouldn't wonder if he just sat there and waited for me to pity him.

Approval and sympathy.

He's come to ask me for approval and sympathy.

I can't believe it.

But none of these thoughts showed on Lenore's clear brow, and that little twist of her mouth, it too was gone by the time she answered the doorbell.

They stood there for a few seconds. Awkwardness on his part, infinite patience on hers. He could see the light coming in through the window just behind her, could see little speckles of dust glimmering between the plants. He could see the shine on her hair. But he couldn't smell it, never had much of a nose, which was very fortunate for him. For in her shampoo Lenore always included a fragrance so balmy, so ambrosial, many a man had lost his mind just trying to smell her hair. But Layla's husband, he was safe as far as Lenore's shampoo was concerned. He was safe from all those alluring aromas that emanated from her body, from behind her ears, those sneaky vapors that could have enveloped him in a cloud of stupefaction in no time at all.

He did step in finally. Looking just a bit neater than

ever, Lenore thought, yet without his usual tie. She noticed this detail with great satisfaction. She always liked her predictions to come true.

"So," she said, hardly giving him time to find a seat. "So," she consciously repeated, just as he was sinking into her sofa, off balance, as it were.

"Well," he said, which, again, seemed just the right thing for him to do, especially with that long, lingering silence afterwards. He wasn't even looking about, he was just sitting there, stone-still, minute after minute. She could feel him freezing up her sofa, and she knew very well that had she been just a bit different, just a bit shakier—just a bit—she would have frozen inside just watching him, seeing the way his body sank into the pale leather around him, the stiffness of his cheeks, the steaming stillness of his eyes. But fortunately, she wasn't shaky. She wasn't any different at all. And he felt it only too well, with those violet eyes resting so calmly on him.

He shifted in his seat. "I really don't know what to do about Layla," he blurted.

This wasn't going as planned for him, he had never been as successful with his plans as Lenore. He had never had her acute eye, which taught her what to expect at every turn of event. Quite the contrary, things slipped by him by the minute.

"I don't know what to do," he repeated. He was going for the sincere, disarming approach, going about it all wrong, actually, considering his audience.

"I thought she'd stop the flying by now," he mumbled. "When she came back from Alaska and she didn't fly anywhere all those weeks, I thought it was over.

"Of course it's quite all right with me if she wants to fly," he quickly added, and no amount of words will help us settle the question of his sincerity. "But what about the girls? And there's other people. People are starting to notice. I really don't know what to do."

Now Lenore knew very well this couldn't count as a question. He's just complaining, she said to herself. He just wants me to know how difficult my sister has become. Good for her. But until he asks me a question he certainly won't hear an answer, she thought, which was a very trivial thought for her to have. She never did speak unless directly required to, or unless she just felt like it. So she offered him some coffee. Surely no rudeness was called for.

"Do you take sugar?" she asked, "And how about milk?"

"No sugar, no milk, thank you."

He liked this. He was glad of these simple questions, and he was always glad to have some of Lenore's coffee, which had a special, sharp wakefulness to it.

So she brought him a cup and he took it, hardly touching her skin as she passed it to him, which again, was very fortunate for him.

"So," she said again, an edge of boredom in her voice. His silences might freeze little sister, she thought, but they will soon send me right back to sleep.

He was getting angry again. He had counted on some help. Yes, he knew Lenore would be difficult, but she did care for her sister, and, well, one could have expected her to show some interest.

"What do *you* think about it?" he asked.

The ball is in her court now, he thought with naive satisfaction.

"I don't think of it very much, really," replied Lenore, and in her case, the sincerity was indisputable. Painfully so. She really did have other concerns, and aside from general approval, her sister's flying didn't interest her as much as one could wish. Even the scooter itself didn't excite her beyond its amusement value. She had her own ways of going places, and this childish contraption seemed, well, just a bit childish.

Just a bit like Layla.

"No, I guess you don't," the husband grudgingly admitted. Or was he being sarcastic? He was certainly becoming angrier and angrier by the minute. "I guess it's no concern of yours that your sister is making such a bloody fool of herself. I guess you don't care if other people think she's crazy or if they think she's just sleeping around. I guess you don't care that your nieces woke up this morning and asked if Mommy had come back already. As if a flying mother were the most normal thing one could have."

"I wouldn't mind a flying mother," said Lenore.

"Oh I'm sure you wouldn't. You wouldn't mind it if your mother were as strange as could be, you wouldn't mind if people called her a whore or a witch. For all I know, maybe she *was* a witch. I wouldn't wonder at all, considering."

Oh, he was angry now. He could see the shrug hidden in her shoulder, that mocking arch just waiting at the tip of her eyebrow. He almost knew how pompous he looked to her, how pompous she actually made him seem. That smoothness of her hair, that cool sharp edge of her cheekbone, it made him all sore with anger. Clearly she was making fun of him—and enjoying it, too. With not a thought for his own pain, for his own lonely nights, not a single thought for him of any kind at all.

Oh, he was angry. Still glued to his chair, still rigid around the jowls, but so, so angry. What a monster he became now, what a furious, horrid monster. A monster of a thousand angry faces. You don't really have to try and imagine this monster. Bad dreams, that's what it would give you. That face, so red, and the lips, tight and pale. And that cold, frozen look in thousands of glistening eyes, as mean as a winter dawn.

I've done it now, haven't I? Frightened you just a bit, perhaps reminded you of a face you once saw, not in your sleep even, no; on the street, say, or just around your own house. But I have promised not to alarm you. I really don't wish to trouble your sleep, not with a simple furious monster. So, you've had all you need of the husband's wicked transformation. I know you can imagine the rest of it. Remember how angry he was. And this, after all, was his wife's sister, who had probably encouraged her to go on those crazy trips of hers, who had probably planted the evil, restless seed. Who had teased him for years now.

And Lenore, what about her eyes? Had they changed? No dearest. Not quite yet. Violet, deep, empty violet; mute violet. Curious violet. Patient violet, that's what they were. Just waiting for his anger to waste away, as would certainly happen, for that's the way of anger, no matter how fierce. Which, by the way, is something quite useful to remember.

So she sat there, and she let him pour out his maddened heart. His tiny, stingy heart, she thought. And he did, he did, talking not only of Layla's scooter and Layla's trips, but of Layla as such, Layla of the hurried feet and clumsy hands, Layla the gazing, Layla the yearning, all those irksome years of yearning he had done nothing to deserve. "I never figured out what it is that she wants," he concluded. "Some say flowers would do the trick, but I doubt it."

"Have you ever tried?" Lenore purred.

"Certainly not. Layla isn't that kind of a fool. Oh no. She couldn't be the regular kind of fool, your sister. She's made up a foolishness that's all her own."

No she hasn't, thought Lenore; not until recently. You'd be surprised to know what a regular kind of fool my sister always was, only you never even tried the flowers, did you.

She was speaking out loud now. "You never even tried. You were too lazy for that even. You just sat there and watched her bump into walls, and you never even tried. You just waited for her to freeze. And you almost did, you almost froze my sister to death. But now, now you're worried, aren't you? She's not doing all her silly smiles for you anymore. She actually looks like something is troubling her, and you want to take that look off her face. You're all alike, all the nasty lot of you!"

Her eyes were all wild and blue now, cyanide blue, paralyzing blue, a blue he'd never seen before.

"Well I won't let you," she shrieked, "I won't let you do it!" Her hair was now flying about her face, and then—in! in!—went her nails—in!—she dug with her claws, looking for that little, shrivelled heart of his.

It came out with a plop, just as always, so quick he hardly even noticed it. He just said a rude word or two and fled.

And Lenore, she held the heart in her palm, tossed and caught it a couple of times, just for fun.

He didn't deserve a heart, he certainly didn't, not after letting her sister freeze inside all those years, letting her walk about in those shabby clothes, letting her wince with disappointment from dawn to dusk.

He deserves no better, thought Lenore. Layla will thank me for this some day.

And she put the heart in one of her special jars and labeled it, as neatly as always, "Layla's husband, November 3, 1998."

A warm shower now, a long warm shower and she'd be just fine. Let the soapy water rinse off that strange stench that always came from such work as hers. Special soap, soap her dear, wise aunt had taught her to make. Jars and jars of soaps and lotions, perfumes and ointments, all neatly labeled. She had worked hard to get them, that's for sure.

But Lenore wasn't tired, not at all. She wasn't tired and she wasn't upset, and she certainly wasn't impressed. She had her creams to take care of that, didn't she? So after her long, warm shower, after shampooing the smell out of her hair and after taking great, tender care of her body, Lenore wrapped herself in yet another clean sheet, and lazily waltzed about the room with that secret smile on her lips.

"You shouldn't have done it," said Luna, melting in through one of the walls.

"Shouldn't have done what?" replied Lenore, without missing even one beat of her waltz. But the smile vanished. It was a smile for men only, remember.

"You shouldn't have stolen his heart," insisted earnest little Luna. "Who knows what he will do now?"

"I'll tell you what he will do. Nothing, that's what. He won't even know that it's gone. Hasn't used it in years. And look how small it is. Have you ever seen such a small one?" Lenore opened the jar, which she had held all along in her waltzing hand.

"I don't want to look. You know how these things hurt me," said Luna, and indeed she doubled up with pain, that old, cold pain, which had gripped her inside ever since her childhood, whenever she felt the Loveless Winds approach.

"I'm sorry, oh Luna sweetie, I'm really sorry," said Lenore, and she carefully hugged her sister, her little sister. It always pained her to see her little sister's pain, only she never could see it coming in advance. All those lotions and creams, especially the Anti-Wrinkle/No Troubles one, the one she had had as far back as she could remember, they had made her eyelids a bit heavy, just a bit slow, especially where the Loveless Winds were concerned.

"Perhaps it was small," Luna cried, "but it was there. And now, who knows what he will do? How could you? Just like that, for the fun of it, without even a thought for Layla, and the girls, all alone with him, who knows what he will do now, Lenore? How could you, how could you do it, just like that, as if it were one more game for you to play, one more jar to fill and label? You must be mad, Lenore, completely and horribly mad. I tell you, we shall all pay for this. You have ruined us, Lenore, and you've danced your little waltz on our grave."

Never, never had Lenore heard her sister use so many words at a time. Never had she heard Luna so angry. Never had she heard a reproach fall from those quiet lips, and this new voice of hers, this hollow crescendo—bitter, foreboding—what had she done to earn it?

Oh god, what had she done, how could she, how could she have done it, how awfully stupid? But she'd fix it, she would.

"I'll fix it, Luna," Lenore promised, with all her heart. "I'll put it back, or I'll do something else, I don't know what, but I promise I'll fix it. You'll see."

Did Luna really believe her?

Did she really think Lenore could fix what seemed so unfixable?

Perhaps she did.

Maybe she didn't.

But she stopped crying.

Perhaps she realized crying wouldn't make a difference.

"Only think this time," said Luna, her voice back to

tender. "Just think this time. Things have gone very wrong, Lenore, more than you know perhaps. Do think, Lenore, think carefully."

Good advice.

And Lenore really meant to follow it.

11
the dance
of treason

On and on she waltzed, on and on, no mirrors there to catch her ever fearful eye, no reflection called for at all. No mirrors, none of them, even that three-doored cabinet had disappeared. There was nothing there to reflect her lovely image, and yet . . .

As Layla waltzed on, as she twirled and swirled about, passing on from partner to partner, as dazzling as anyone could ever hope to be, a little nagging voice was creeping through the rustly folds of her gown, up, up, over the back of her neck, through her luscious curls, in, in, till it lodged itself safely in her ever-meek ear.

What did that voice say?

Ah, dearest, perhaps you have your guesses, perhaps you could actually imagine yourself there with her—perhaps instead of her. Maybe little voices all your own come seeking you out even as you read. Who knows what your voices are saying? Perhaps you're wishing for a Prince after all, even though you'd have a hard time admitting it—a Prince, in this day and age, with all of us so clever and brave? A Prince? What a thought!

Embarrassing, almost, isn't it?

With curls of his own?

With the smile of Love on his ruby lips?

Wouldn't that mean the castle were his, after all?

No, you do away with that Prince with a flash of a haughty eyebrow, of course you do. You dismiss him from your thoughts. He has become an unpleasant aftertaste in just a few seconds. "Let's not settle for a Prince, Layla!" You want to yell at her, just like you did at the puppet show years and years ago, when you were quite sure every-one was waiting for your guidance.

But perhaps there were other thoughts that passed through that simple mind of Layla's. Two-word thoughts, such as What Next, or What If, and maybe even that hardest of thoughts, What Else, or, to put it differently, What More.

I'll tell you dearest, that little nagging voice managed to say all these things at once. It was amazing, really, how many different things it could say all at once, being such a little voice really, but it could pick up the thinnest strands of anxiety and spin them all into a thread that would lead her, oh, who knows where?

What Next.

How about a Prince. Is one coming?

What Next? Will I stay here forever?
Who Else? Who could come with me?
Could I bring the girls?

Oh the girls, the girls.
Three of them.
All fresh of eye and of heart.
Three little girls, asleep in the dark, breathing so evenly. Three little girls who believed in Wolves and Princes and Mommy too. Little girls who hardly knew what went on once the sun had set, sleeping in their tiny beds, all alone, far away.

Betrayed, when you came right down to it.

Had she? Had she really betrayed them? Would she actually do that? Wasn't that what she considered doing right there and then, dancing so freely, so merrily —surely no one with three little girls could ever dance so freely—even this dancing, wasn't it the dance of treason? Where was Mommy—*oh Mommy*—now? Where was she of the little afternoon walks and bedtime stories? Where was she who would dice up the apples and sprinkle them with raisins? Where was—*oh Mommy*—who could find every little toy as quick as the flash of a tender smile? Here, that's where she was, dancing her feet off, dancing her heart out, dancing her mind quite empty of duty.

But that was just one little strand, wasn't it?

There were others. That Prince did thread his way in, of course he did. Even you would grant her just an occasional thought of a Prince, no matter how childish that may seem; and an occasional thought of the husband, her husband, that slow chilly husband of seven years, so solid, so immovable, so utterly, utterly fixed; and her sisters, her sisters, too, the lot of them. What would they say? Would they like to be right here with her? She would like that, wouldn't she? Even if it were just to show them her palace, to show them how lovely she had become, to let them see all these people, all looking at her with such admiration. She'd want her sisters to see that, wouldn't she?

Perhaps she wouldn't, actually.

There was that, too, spun right in there with all the rest. Perhaps she wouldn't want them there at all. She could imagine their smiles, especially Liora and Lenore, each with her own shade of derision. "Any good fucks?" Lenore would ask, just to tease her, just to mock this beautiful ball she was having in her very own castle. Liora, well, she would be standing there, not one to be swept off her feet, not at all. She would take it all in and then ask about breakfast or say something about the treacherous ways of magic.

But Lihi would join in the dance.

Lihi would.

She wouldn't be properly dressed, perhaps, but she would dance, and her smile would be wide open.

As for Luna, oh Luna, what a steady strand of pain.

Luna.

How could she forget little Luna, who never even had the tiniest bit of this.

Shame, shame on her for forgetting Luna.

She had become treacherous indeed.

Now the ways of dealing with nagging voices are many, but this little voice, the one of so many strands, well, Layla dealt with it in her own way, which was picking one strand and quickly dropping it, moving from one to another, never following any one of them too far. Careful, that's what she was, always had been. She wouldn't let any one of these strands entangle her in meshes of pain, not our Layla, Layla of the many smiles, smiles for all troubles and occasions. No pain would ever touch her heart—it had been promised, it had been paid for and settled. Surely it was a bit late in the day to change all of that. And who on earth would want to.

Yet . . . Even though she dropped those strands so quickly, so deftly, they did slow her down just a bit. Her feet felt a bit heavy after all those hours of care-free dancing.

It was time to go home again.

What else?

So she called on her scooter, and she called on the elf too. Just to thank him. There was no reason to forget politeness just because he was en elf—quite the contrary, Layla was sure extra politeness was called for, you see. She had been taught that politeness was the best and only way to make your way in this world, the best way to keep your hard-earned possessions.

So she just told him, "I have to go back now, and thank you ever so much for all this."

"Won't there be anything else?" asked the earnest elf, and this question kept hovering about her, even as she flew home, even as she made lunch and dinner and all those other things that had become too ordinary to think about.

Let alone mention.

Won't there be anything else?

Not necessarily, thought Layla as she pecked her husband on the cheek. Not necessarily, she thought, as she dreamily put the laundry in the washer. Not necessarily, not at all. It was a wonderful deal she had now, it really was.

It could go on and on forever.

Or so she thought.

Because once again, Layla forgot all those other people around her. The husband's new heartlessness, for instance. She didn't even notice it. Sure, the air about him was chilly, it shrouded him like the darkest of dark gowns, but chilliness had settled in their house long ago. And she wasn't watching his every look, not as carefully as she should have, not anymore. Indeed, she made a point of it, after seven years of searching his face for any trace of passion.

And it had been such a small heart, anyway.

It was hard to tell, even if you hadn't just spent the whole night waltzing.

Of course there were the girls. Just a bit alarmed, that's what they were. They knew Mommy had spent the night away. They had seen their father's white nostrils in the morning, and in that still, quiet house, the little house of the twisted passages, such whiteness proclaimed itself as loud as any scream. But they were small, and the trouble, oh, it was getting bigger and bigger, so big they couldn't even start guessing at it. They only cried just a bit more than usual and asked for an extra lullaby. (No, not that other lullaby. Layla had never ever made any deal for them. She did know enough to leave the Winds out of their little lives—after all, she had given the Winds enough. She had paid so dearly for her bag of silly smiles, she wouldn't have it happen to her girls. She wouldn't let her girls end up in a chilly house such as hers. So she just sang them simple lullabies of trees and flowers, all gone to sleep along with the clouds and the stars, along with three little dears, whose eyelids drooped so sweetly with every word she sang.)

And then there were her sisters, the lot of them, each thinking her own thoughts about this new adventure that had been thrust upon them—their sister's adventure, for sure, but what did it mean for them? What else would happen? To whom? Who could come along? Who wanted to? What if she went on to adventure-land and left them all behind?

But they weren't talking about it, not really. Not even among themselves.

Not since that party had ended with mouth-rinsing soap.

Each had her own thoughts now. That much had happened already.

That much damage, thought Liora. We were all so close till all this started.

That much good, thought Lenore, who was just slightly fed up with years and years of mint tea.

But Lihi—she just missed her sisters, and more than anything she wanted to hear about Layla's last trip. She wanted to hear all of it.

Only Layla wasn't even calling her.

And of course there was Luna, Luna of the bottom-less eyes, Luna felt a little hope gushing in her, you see. She knew her sister was riding over and above the Winds. She was going places where no Winds could ever reach her. Or so she hoped.

And the elf. Don't forget the elf. There was much more to him than you may think. You've seen him show-ing up here and there, summoned, as it were, by Layla's fleeting wishes, a servant of sorts, really. Maybe that's what you're thinking. And you're right in a way, dearest, but in one way only. You see, the elf too was learning a thing or two as all this went on. He, too, was coming to have thoughts of his own, above the usual scope of elfin thoughts. So many times had this elf granted the wishes of the small-hearted, wishes of fortune and success, wishes of power and beauty. Layla had caught his attention years back in Paris, with that vague, all-inclusive wish of hers. "Oh, I just wish to be happy," she had said, not even try-ing to trick him—a lot of people did that, trying to think of one wish that would cover a lot of ground—but with

Layla you could tell, she really didn't think any one thing counted as such. She just wanted to be happy, and the ways of happiness all seemed alike to her. What with those Loveless Winds, and what with that hollowed-out mother, she didn't even ask for true Love—which was vague and special enough, but not unheard of. No, Layla had just asked for happiness.

It was now occurring to the elf that she had left very much up to him.

Much more than people usually did.

Yet, he didn't really have all the powers one could hope for. He couldn't translate that vague wish into specific form. He couldn't do much more about it than Layla—which had cost her all those many years of false turns and dead-end roads, you see. He always tried to make any minor wish of hers come true, only some of them were of such a weary kind, little bedtime wishes for a good night's sleep, for an easy day, for nice weather even.

As for those dark wishes she would have just before opening her eyes, wishes that too often sounded like, "Oh I just want to have it over and done with"—*it* being marriage at times, or motherhood, or—why not admit it?—*it* sometimes meaning just life, all of it, all the messy lot of it, all that was way too confusing for the elf, who, to tell the truth, was even more simple-minded than she was, even more full of that fairy-tale belief in quick mixes and instant enchantments.

So for quite a few years he had kept away. After all, he did hear Layla speak of her happiness to anyone who would hear. He heard her hum contentedly as she sorted the babies' clothes by size, by season, by color—and he really wasn't one to judge all of this, not at all. Assessing Layla's happiness was way beyond his scope. A lovely girl with stars in her eyes had once told him she wished to be happy. And quite a lovely woman, actually, had avowed for many a year that she was happy indeed, she really was.

If there weren't very many stars in her eyes, if he saw her choose paler and paler shades for her lips, her walls, her dreams—well again, it wasn't the elf's job to argue with Layla about brands of happiness. You have noticed, haven't you, how all those fairies and elves always take you at your word. You'll waste your wish on the silliest nonsense and regret it for the rest of your life, but they never just stand up and say, "Hey, you, don't be such a fool. Save your wish, mend it, ask for a truly good one." No, they'll just let you have it, whatever *it* is. Which is the reason elves got their bad reputation. It does seem a bit spiteful, this way they have of giving you just what it is that you want. It does seem a bit unfair, given how foolish you've been at times. But the truth is, there really is no mean intent in the elves' light-hearted heart. They've never ever pretended to be the conveyors of wisdom. They actually consider them-selves—in a very matter-of-fact light—as the executors of will, technicians, if you like, those who turn dream into reality, those who lead each tale to its nearest end.

But this special elf, presented with such a special kind of Layla, one who hardly even understood what it was one could wish for, one who seemed to turn about and flee every time the occasion rose for a really big wish, he wanted to do something. In his own, elfish way, he wanted to make good. He loved her, you see, with that detached love elves can feel, love that is more like pity, pity for the hardships of men and women, who have so many momentous things to settle in such a fleeting snatch of time.

So he was going to do just that, this wonderful, once-in-a-lifetime elf.

He was going to help Layla make the right wish, just for once. No more laughing shrug, no brushing off—he would make her stand still and wish for something big. Not just a flying scooter, not just little snatches of happiness scattered here and there.

The Real Thing.

Just for once.

But he had to get her to ask for it.

Which would have to take more time, you see. Right at this point, Layla felt almost sure she had enough. It all seemed to do, indeed. She had settled for so much less, and for so long, it didn't seem necessary to ask for anything else. It didn't really seem possible, and it definitely didn't seem wise. Or temperate. Or cautious. Here she was, her girls neatly tucked up in bed, her scooter parked in the garden, her husband just a shade quieter than always—but those shades were too dark to bear close scrutiny anyway—and she had that castle, which seemed to follow her about in some way she couldn't even start guessing at, and there was the elf too, so friendly, so sweet, never ever asking for anything in return, just smiling his little elfish smile, so otherworldly, so ethereal. Layla felt, as she had felt only too often before, that she had everything one could possibly ask for.

And if a little nagging voice inside her mentioned love eternal, love everlasting, overwhelming—well, Layla had lived for so many years in a land of composure, she had been surrounded by such green meadows of ease, she really didn't believe she wished to be overwhelmed.

No sir.

Nice little doses, that's what she wanted.

And she wanted to be in charge of the dosing.

You see, she still wanted to come back in time for lunch, always.

She still had that gift, her bag of smiles, surely she would have to give up on some of them for love over-whelming and all of that. She had tried it once, remember—she herself remembered very well. There were precious few smiles then, no tip-of-the-nose grinning, not at all, just a terribly serious face and a heart full of fear, a heart that kept asking, would it do, would it last, would it? Who could possibly want such a thing? Who could choose to hear all those Winds of Warning, the Winds who always knew all the dangers and had such clever ideas about ways to avoid them?

Which brings us again, oh dearest, to those wily Winds.

Even though we loathe to speak of them.

So what, you may ask, were *they* thinking? What would they do now? What would they do about that scheming elf, who was actually—if perhaps unwittingly—plotting against them?

The ways of the Winds are many, dearest, and we can't be quite sure about their plans.

But one thing we know for certain:

For years and years the Winds had had Layla's words to sing with. For years she had followed their faithless rule. For years and years she had come back to gaze in the mirror, searching for answers, looking at her reflection, seeing the Loveless look hidden deep in her eyes.

They wouldn't want to give up on all of that.

They dreaded that moment when Layla would stop coming to them for answers, when she'd stop that gazing she had learned since childhood, that merciless scrutiny that always left more than enough room for their haunting tune.

For this you must know, dearest: whenever you look with the eyes of true love, whenever you look *into* the eyes of true love, whenever you sink all the way in, not seeking any reflection—as so many do—then you leave the Winds out.

Completely.

Then you leave them wailing their wordless complaint.

Then—only then—are you truly free.

So as long as it was just scooting and waltzing, the Winds could feel quite safe.

Only they knew where all this could lead.

Which is why they had sent Layla all those little animals.

And being quite simple in their own way—for most of us are—they thought, perhaps it is time for a bigger animal. Who knows?

12
all of it

There she was again, with hardly any rest this time, just a few days had passed since her return from Prague.

Hectic, dearest, that's what she was getting.

Greedy, you might say.

But I hope you'll say she's getting serious, at long last. After all this scooting about, after all these little games of magic and enchantment, so many pretend games really, she's finally getting serious.

There she was, surrounded by the most luscious of luscious greens. Green, green, green all over, all possible shades of it and just a few more, hanging above her, trampled beneath her, oh green, green Malaysia, this wasn't white Alaska or tame, civilized Prague, this was the *jungle*, at long last. All those years, when Layla had been dreaming of places to go to—those long-sounding, soft-sounding places that had made her ache with shame for everything she had given up—this was what she had dreamed of. The richness of it. The shrill cries of birds way up in the treetops, the invisible treetops, and the smell, the damp green smell she had always imagined. It was there, too. This was indeed the Jungle of her dreams, and here she was, Layla of the careful steps and the neat stacks of laundry, brave at last. Surely this was as brave as anyone could get, one woman with a scooter, all alone in all this wild richness.

"I wonder, would you care for a ride," someone purred right behind her.

Layla turned about sharply. She hadn't counted on hearing any animals this time, she thought she had done away with all those irksome little creatures.

Only this one wasn't so little.

This was a panther, a full-sized black panther, grinning at her just enough to reveal his white fangs.

Was she alarmed?

Well yes, just a bit.

But she wouldn't let it show. Not if her life depended on it.

You see, she had a very clear idea by now, simpleminded though she may have been, why all those animals kept coming her way.

And she wasn't all that simple-minded by now.

"So where would you like to take me?" she asked. Cool as a cucumber, she thought. Cool as the coolest cucumber indeed. No one, no one is going to frighten me now, not even a talking panther. Definitely not a talking panther.

Did she start sobbing hysterically, now that there was no one to impress?

The answer is yes to the trembling, but even that just for the shortest while. And not even one sob escaped her pursed lips.

Determined, that's what she had become. Surprisingly, incredibly, belatedly determined. And just a bit impatient, too. So many ways and days of waiting, so many weeks and years of doubting, so much questioning and gazing, she wanted to be done with it. She was done with it, surely.

"I've actually done away with a panther, haven't I?" she said, quite proud of herself. "If I'm not quite mistaken, this is where the elf should come in."

Cool as a cucumber indeed. Cool as champagne, cool as the freshest morning rain, cool as anyone could ever wish to be

"Here I am, dearest," said the elf. "You were quite incredible there, you really were."

"Yes I was, wasn't I?" Layla replied, all composed by now, actually humming. "It was easier than ever before, really. And you know, even though he did give me quite a scare, I actually enjoyed myself. Oh sweet, sweet elf, isn't this quite wonderful! I wish I could stay here forever!"

"I'd be glad to arrange that," the elf replied, as prompt as a salesman.

"You really could, couldn't you?" Layla said, and he could tell by the look she gave him that she was finally seeing the glimmering peak of Wishland.

"I'd have to think about that," she slowly said, with not a trace of a giggle in her voice.

"This is a good moment for thinking," replied the elf, who unlike some of his mischievous fellow elves would never dream of acting upon an "I wish" sentence that hadn't been meant as such.

"You really can make my every wish come true?" Layla asked, as if she saw him fully for the first time now.

"Each and every one of them," said the elf. "But you have to ask."

Now if this had happened just one year earlier, Layla would have actually grumbled. "Who ever heard of such a thing?" she would have said. "You can't really mean it," she would have said. "Not each and every, surely not, maybe one, or three, or any other agreed-upon number, but not each and every." She would have called her sisters, for sure. She would have checked with them.

Had they ever, ever heard of such a spree of wish-granting?

Could this elf be trusted?

Could this be considered cautious?

And what about Temperance?

But this was happening now in Malaysia. It wasn't happening in Paris, when the mere act of wishing had seemed too much of a challenge, and it wasn't even happening one year ago, when a grumble and a snigger would have sent the elf away as quick as a slap in the face. No, this was happening now, and Layla had given up her grumbling and sniggering. She had foregone all that for the longest while now.

So when the elf answered, so earnestly, so magnificently, Layla finally understood how serious this was.

"And it's not just one wish, or three?" she asked, just

to make sure. Perhaps it wouldn't be so hard if there were a whole sack of wishes to draw from.

"It isn't really about numbers," said the elf. "It's about good wishes. I only want to do the good ones."

Layla felt a throb of exasperation fleeting across her eyebrows. "You did say 'each and every,' you know," she reminded him.

"I can never be cross with you," was the elf's gallant reply. But he could have pointed out to her that literal interpretations were quite a double-edged sword, and he hadn't taken her for her word just a little while ago.

Meanwhile, Layla was trying to outdo herself. She wasn't going to argue, she definitely wasn't going to stand there in all that greenery and argue with a real elf who was waiting for her every wish. Obviously she would have to relax about this. He said he would give her any good wish she asked for.

So it was time for a wish.

A really good one.

"I'll have that Prince now," she quickly mumbled, somewhat shyly, somewhat majestically, and thoroughly embarrassed. After all, everyone expected her to ask for a Prince. Surely even the elf had meant just that, not that she wanted to be childish or anything, not that she thought it was the best of all possible wishes, not that she would have asked for one if the elf had been more strict about numbers, but under the circumstances, and having that castle already, and the scooter, and the long hair that always streamed along her back when she flew anywhere, well, a Prince seemed a very snug kind of wish. "Just don't make it too silly, please," she quickly added. "I don't mean a crown or a cape, or anything like that."

"I know just what you mean, dearest, please don't worry. I wouldn't ever do anything to embarrass you," said the elf.

With those words he disappeared, just as the coziest of rooms materialized around her.

In it, just standing there, smiling at her with the kindest of kind smiles, was her Prince.

Oh dearest, dearest, please don't ask me to tell you very much of that Prince. He was Layla's Prince after all, and perhaps you yourself wouldn't have known him for one. But Layla did, you see. And she would have known him with or without the elf, with or without that magic room. She would have known him at first sight, quick as love.

Which made her cry rather terribly, so happy she was to feel those comforting arms about her.

You'd like to know just what happened there?

You'd like to know what sweet words and tender embraces were exchanged?

All of them, dearest, the best and rightest words and embraces, that's what.

As good as a wish come true.

And did they live happily ever after?

How could they?

There were still three little girls, about to wake up in their beds.

No one had ever told Layla a tale of a Princess and a Prince and three little girls.

So she couldn't quite tell how it was supposed to end.

She left him there, asleep in their very own chamber. It wasn't so hard to leave him when he was asleep.

And it was time for breakfast, after all.

The Prince could wait.

As always.

He could stay there, in that room, sweetly asleep till she woke him up with her kisses. He'd remain there, steady as a wish, and she, Princess Layla, she would come and go as she pleased, because that was the kind of Princess she could be. That was the kind she chose to be, as enchanted as she pleased, as ordinary. She could be a day-and-night sort of changeling princess—after all, she was the Flying Princess, she had mastered the best magic of all: the magic of Back and Forth.

Oh dear, dear, dearest, imagine Layla's face as she walked in through the silent door of that little house, no tip-of-the-nose smile, no smile at all, just a dreamy look of pleasure nestling in her eyes, just a peaceful shade of pink on her face and a certain bounce in her step.

Anyone could tell.

Anyone could tell, but the husband didn't.

He had other things on his mind now.

He had his mind all set by now.

A long lonely night had set it for him.

A steady, heartless rage had made it all clear. How could she? Just back from Prague and off again, with not a word to anyone this time, as if she expected them all to dance to her silly little tune, as if she really thought he'd settle for hasty breakfasts and sloppy shirts. Well, he wouldn't, he couldn't. He was a father of three and a man of the world. No one, no one would pull this scooting act on him, certainly not his wife. And if that shade of pink had warmed his heart just a few weeks ago, if that peace in her eye had actually made him glad then, well, things were all different now. He didn't quite know why and how, of course he didn't. He only knew Layla couldn't do this to him anymore. She couldn't just come and go as she pleased.

And he actually said so.

In so many words, and many more.

He'd have no more of it, he said. No scooter, no flying, possibly no sisters. He'd have her stay put. And if she was restless, well, she could find things to do. He didn't expect her to stay home all day, it was she who had said that it made her so happy. It was she who said she didn't want anything else, and if she did want other things now, well very fine, but they'd have to be accessible by car.

And there was an "Or Else," dearest, of course there was. There always is after such passionate words.

And this was such a big "Or Else," it made Layla turn quite deaf.

Or Else he'd take the girls, he said.

And he went into that little syllogism about whores

and madwomen and witches, all of which led to one cruel bottom line.

Custody.
All of it.
All just for him.
Things like that could be arranged, he said. Especially with a mother of three who felt entitled to scoot about whenever she pleased.

A little deaf, that's what she went.
Custody?
All of it?
Who ever heard of such a cruel, heartless thing? Who could ever hear it? Not our Layla, she who had combed and cuddled, who had fed and bathed so perfectly, who had sorted clothes for all seasons and reasons, she wasn't one to hear all this talk. Not our Layla, who had learned to wrap up any trouble with a quick smile, and always, always got away with it.

Couldn't she have guessed, you ask, shouldn't she have known what would happen?

Perhaps she should have, but she certainly didn't.

Not with that easy, almost lazy habit of hers, of dropping any strand of thought that became too hot to handle, dropping it so quickly she never even had to notice it. How could she let such knowledge be admitted? Not our Layla, our simple-minded, sweet-minded

Layla. Why, if she had, she'd never have gotten that scooter to fly.

No, there was just no way she could have known, and she wasn't quite sure she could know even now. Not at all. Why, she had a squinting smile ready for just such hardships, a big mushy clown smile, with her eyes almost perfectly shut. No one, no one would find her behind that smile of hers. No trouble could seep in through it.

This smile also said the following: This was her husband, after all.

She knew him by heart.

She'd earned such knowledge after seven years of freezing within.

Surely seven years of freezing had earned her this right. Surely she could smile him off even though she felt the fright racing up to her face. Surely she should smile even harder, now that her cheeks were burning with fear.

Nothing would make him give up his quiet morning coffee, said her little smile. Nothing would make him rush about and take care of all those things he now claimed could be taken care of.

Yet, even as she looked at him with eyes newly defiant, eyes that had gazed at him for so long in vain, eyes that had just beheld a Prince, as real as anyone could ever wish for, she knew he actually meant every word he said. She could see it by that white rim at the base of his flaring nostrils, that familiar, angry redness in his face. She could see how set his mind was, and she knew just how incredibly set that could be.

He actually meant it.

And he didn't even know about that new complication, that sweet-eyed Prince lying there, waiting for her. She hoped he didn't know about him at all. It was just the scooter, as far as he was concerned, and he wanted her to give it up. Right away, he had said.

Or Else.

Did she really think he could do it? Did she really believe he could just take those three little girls away?

Of course she did, dearest.

She truly believed this could be, and she truly believed it couldn't.

Which was just another reason for her deafness, wasn't it?

Because she knew, she had known all along. Because she really wasn't surprised at all, no matter how deaf she went. Because she had always believed she'd be found out some day, some day all that bright-eyed Mommying would be seen for what it was. Some day that queer sadness inside her would make itself known. Some day she would be found out. Some day the bag of smiles would be all used up. And the day, it seemed, had finally come.

But she also knew this: she wouldn't be stopped now. No way. Not after all those doubts and qualms which had taken so long to settle. Not after she had almost bored herself to death. Yes, bored to death—who said boredom was a childish thing to complain about, what the cruel Winds had made her put up with? How boring, how utterly boring he had always been. No, she wouldn't have it. She had earned her scooter by seven years of patient waiting, seven years of mild horror and fierce disillusion, seven years of fumbling and bumping through those twisted passages. She had earned it, and no one, no one would take it away from her.

Oh dire, dire predicament. Her own lovely daughters, fresh as strawberries, sweet as cream, with eyes that sang of love from dawn to dusk. Surely she couldn't give them up. Surely no one could expect her to do that, no one could ever, ever set anyone up for such a horrible choice.

"How awful," Lihi said, when her sister tearfully called her. "Are you sure you can't make him change his mind?" Which question made Layla feel lonelier than ever. After all, she had never, ever told any of her sisters how set the husband's mind could be. She couldn't really expect them to know about that glistening threat twinkling in his eye whenever he was finally sure about something.

But when Lihi asked, "Couldn't you use the bracelet?" then Layla went all quiet inside. Why, the thought had never occurred to her, never once. With a rush of hope she dug into her treasure chest, where the bracelet was always hidden between trips. She took it out, that golden bracelet of seven charms, and for a moment she wondered, could she really whoosh him away?

She tried, dearest. She was frantic enough to try, even though she knew it wouldn't work. How could it, when the husband loomed so over her heart, larger and larger by the minute? Of course it wouldn't work, it couldn't, not that bracelet for little disturbances and mild troubles, that weird gift, as tricky as any other gift the Winds ever give. And Layla, she wasn't even disappointed, not really, even as she shook those charms she knew just how feeble they were when faced with trouble so solid.

"Why does it have to be such a tragedy?" asked Lenore on the phone, smoothing back her cool, smooth hair. "Who said it had to be this big, all-time, all-or-nothing choice? Why do you have to be so simple, Layla? You can have your girls part time, shared time, whatever. I always thought they were a bit much for you. Three of them, for God's sake. What were you thinking of, Layla? Didn't you see what it did to Mother, having so many of us? Didn't she frighten you at all?"

"It's your choice," said Liora that evening, "but you can't have it all, that's for sure. He won't let you." And of course there was some wise talk of the having and eating of cakes, of two-ended sticks and the only way of making an omelet.

"It really is your choice," the Winds sang in her ear all day long, and they'd put on little shows just for her. They'd have the curtains flapping with foreboding in the girls' room. They'd tear the laundry off the line, no matter how neatly and carefully she hung it, which was even neater and more careful than before.

Layla had tried so hard, and for so long, to keep everything in its rightful place—the laundry, the toys, even the girls. No door had been slammed in that house for seven years, no creak had been heard, everything was as still as could be. As it should be, Layla thought.

No more. Now the Winds were shaking it all up, mocking her attempts at order. Her hair, the papers on her desk, everything was flying about as wild as could be, and they'd toy with the girls' hair, whose tidiness had always been such a source of motherly pride. By the time evening finally came to that poor, bewildered household, Layla actually found herself yelling at the little one, "What have you done with your hair? You look like you've been pulling it five different ways all at once, you naughty, naughty child. No wonder it hurts when I'm combing it." And indeed she brushed harder than ever, she had to get that hair back into place if it was the last thing she did. Surely no one could come and mess up her little girls like that. And if the little one cried, well, what of it? Layla would show everyone just what a good mother she could be, scooter or no scooter. What were they all thinking? Of course she'd stay with her girls, husband or no husband, prince or no prince. She'd never, ever leave them.

Only that was said in the evenings, when the lights in the girls' room were dim, when they were lying in their little beds, sweet and warm after their bath. But there were mornings, too, bitter, sharp mornings, and we haven't even mentioned the nights yet, with the husband still there.

Who could be so cruel, she thought, who could give me my castle and my Prince and then make me give up on my girls. It isn't fair, she thought, and she didn't need the mocking Winds to tell her just how childish she was being.

But we mustn't rush now, dearest. We mustn't rush just because we feel something whirling about us, something with a whiff of an end to it, perhaps. We mustn't rush, and we mustn't peek ahead, we must carefully listen to what happened next.

Because indeed it occurred to more than one person, that the scooter's rightful place wasn't under that pine tree at all.

Liora, Lenore, the husband—it could be anyone of them, couldn't it, dearest, who would decide to steal that troublesome, awesome little scooter.

Because it was stolen.

As Layla found out one morning, when her wailing woke up the whole neighborhood.

"What happened to the scooter?" you ask, your eyes round with worry.

Stolen, dearest, just as I've said.

And if you want to know why, or by whom, we'll have to retrace our steps just a bit. We'll have to return to ten-thirty on the night of Layla's trip to Malaysia.

To the long, lonely night the husband had spent in the living-room.

When that cold, heartless rage started welling inside him.

Just because this was a rage so heartless, he could still remember his overall plan.

A civilized, rational demeanor.

To be attested to by his wife's own sisters, if ever the need for attesting should arise.

So he called Liora, once more.

Only this time he didn't fumble. This time there were no "uh's" and "hmm's." "I'm going to put an end to this," he said.

"You are?" Liora said, actually surprised.

"I definitely am," he said. "I'll have your dear sister know she has to stop flying about. I'll have her know the price should she continue."

"You aren't going to leave her, are you?" said Liora, almost incredulous.

"There won't be any need for that," he calmly replied. "If she wants to keep up this insane flying, I'll find a place for her. Somewhere where she can get help. She needs it. And the girls need a life that's normal, with or without their mother. They can't be told of flying scooters. They can't wake up and wonder whether Mommy has shown up for breakfast. I have to think of them, you know. And right now, unless she decides to stop all this foolery, they're better off without her. These things can be taken care of, you know."

For ten whole seconds Liora was speechless.

"You can't do that! I'm sure you wouldn't do that, not to Layla. Hasn't she always come back in time? Why on earth would you take the girls? How could you be so heartless?"

He didn't answer that. "I've made up my mind," he insisted. "I do hope Layla will be sensible, but if she isn't, well, I don't see there's anything else left for me to do."

And it was Liora who hung up, as flustered as she had been in years.

When had all this happened, was what she wanted to know. She wouldn't ever, ever have thought him capable of such ruthless obstinacy, not this quiet, slow man whom she knew for over seven years now. Who would have ever guessed?

So she asked Lenore to come over.

And they had a little talk about it (though no mention was made of that swift plucking. Only Luna knew about that.)

They called in Lihi, too, just for the record.

And it was decided, right there between them:

Their sister really needed help now.

They couldn't take any risks.

The scooter had to go.

Did they all agree about it, just like that? Did they all believe the husband's threats?

No to the first dearest, but yes to the second. Lenore knew what she knew, and she persuaded all of them—without going into too many facts—that something had to be done. After all, if Layla agreed to stop flying, it wouldn't even matter.

And if she didn't, well, they'd be doing her a favor really. She couldn't actually prefer to lose her girls.

To tell the truth, Liora actually thought the husband had a point, a bit of a point at least. The scooter wasn't doing her sister any good at all.

How about Lihi, you ask, how about young, carefree Lihi? Didn't she find all of this just a bit underhanded?

Didn't she want her sister to go on flying? Of course she did, but she was the youngest, after all. She hadn't ever argued any point with her sisters, certainly not with Liora and Lenore, who seemed to agree this time as never before. And what did she know about it? Who was she to say?

As for Luna, silent Luna—Luna who wouldn't have ever agreed to such cold-bloodedness, poor little Luna, who heard the Winds hum about those conspiring sisters—she didn't quite know what to think. All those years she had helped her sisters go through their loveless days, and she'd come for her soothing visits at night. But this was new. This dangerous, heartless husband, and Layla, so hopeful, so rosy, so desperate, it was all so new, so different, who could tell what would happen next? So she looked at her sisters with those grave eyes, and quietly nodded. "Maybe it's time," said Luna. "This will hurt Layla horribly, but perhaps it wouldn't be so bad for pain to touch her heart."

As for Lenore, remember she had promised Luna to make up for that rash impulse of her nails and her cyanide eyes. And no one had ever taught her how to mend a heart.

And there was also this: Lenore really believed that scooter was ridiculous. She wanted her sister to fly, but not like that.

And as she looked at herself in the mirror, and as she toyed with her lovely smooth hair, she heard a breezy voice telling her: "Go ahead, you'll be doing her a favor."

And so, after a few days had passed, and no one heard any further word from Layla, they decided the moment had come.

In the stealthy still of the night, dressed in black just as ever, Lenore made her way to her sister's house, straight to the pine tree, where the patient scooter stood, waiting. And she lifted it carefully, silently, and put it in the back of her car.

There.

She had done the right thing.

She had fixed what needed fixing.

Layla would thank her for it some day.

13
to face a
mockingbird

Oh, how she wailed.

Neighbors, hardly ever seen in that quiet, shady neighborhood, peeked out of their windows.

It sounded as if someone had just died.

It sounded as if someone's child had died.

And it didn't stop.

A grown woman was standing in her yard, wailing her heart out.

She had only wanted one last trip.

To say her last goodbye.

To get one last hug.

To have something to remember for years and years, something to dream about at night, in that chilly bed that would now be hers forever.

And she wanted the scooter to remain there, always. Reminding her.

Poor Layla, who had just recently remembered how to hope.

She walked back into the house.

It was all over.

The trips, that rush of air about her when she rose on her scooter—Malaysia, Alaska, Prague—it was all over. The castle, the queendom she had felt for the first time in her life, all gone, taken from her who knows why, perhaps because she had already made up her mind. Because she had frightened so easily. And the Prince, that wonderful Prince, how would she ever find him now? She had given up on him years and years ago. She had thought him but a silly dream until she saw him standing there with that loving gladness in his smile. What would she do now? How could she live for even one more day with all that bitter longing in her heart?

All over.

With not one last word of farewell.

Unless . . .

"Oh elf, come, come, please come," she cried.

And he did.

Of course he did.

"What can I do for you, Layla?" he asked, as meek as the meekest genie.

"Could you take me to my castle just for once, just this last time, please?" she asked, all blind with tears.

"Open your eyes, sweet Layla. Look."

The elf was gone. And the Prince was there, waiting, asleep.

Layla decided to wait just a bit before waking him. She'd walk her castle for one last time. She'd say goodbye to those splendorous halls. She'd even step out and see just where the castle stood this time.

Green Malaysia, of course. She hadn't mentioned any other place.

With a heart heavy with delight and regret all mingled in a painful jumble, Layla walked among the trees. A sweet chirping caught her ear. She turned, and there, on a branch quite close to her, the mockingbird preened its feathers.

"Too good to be true, ha?" the mockingbird chirped.

But Layla didn't even answer.

There wasn't any point, really.

And after all, that silly bird was right.

So she walked back in, back to that fragrant chamber where her Prince now stood, clear of eye and heart, expecting her.

She'd spend the day with him.

She'd stay the night.

This was the last time, after all.

And what a time it was, a lifetime of joy packed into that day and that night, soothing, soothing balm, touching every ache she had ever felt, almost making up for all the time wasted, all the time yet to be lost. There wasn't even time for fear now, nothing to stop that flow of infinite tenderness, tenderness all-embracing, tenderness eternal, if not everlasting. There was no time for giggling or sniggering, none at all, only that wondrous feeling of dreams come absolutely true.

Along with endless waves of pain.

Along with the sweet knowledge, that for once, at least, no bag of smiles was called for. For once, at least, she knew just what it meant to feel your heart burst with love.

Surely that would be enough to take her through a lifetime, if only as a memory.

Surely that would do away with all questions about her heart, her own cautious heart, the heart that had always been so fearful. It did know how to do the best kind of love, if only given a chance.

There had to be some comfort in that knowledge.

Layla fell asleep next to her Prince, even though she hadn't meant to. She had meant to spend the night watching him, carefully memorizing him. For future reference, as it were. But that flow of tenderness, that sweet, glad love, it made her so soft inside, so clear and easy, it didn't leave any room for care.

It made her fall asleep, right there beside him.

Morning rose, and yet Layla slept.

She slept till that mocking chirp aroused her.

"Too good to be true, you know that," the mocking-bird hooted. "Too good for real life, scooter or no scooter. Did you really think that rusty scooter could take you up and away from it all? How high did you think it could fly, you silly Layla?"

But Layla, awake now, with just a few moments to spare, had no time for this.

"It isn't too good to be true," she said. "It could have been true."

"Not for you it couldn't," the mockingbird screeched. "Not for your timid little heart. Perhaps for someone else. Someone else would have stayed here, you know. Someone else would have just stayed. You did say love overwhelm-ing, didn't you? Well, you don't seem so overwhelmed to me, no you don't, with all those little peeks at your watch. You still plan to be home for breakfast, right? That kind of planning doesn't go very well with this kind of love, you know. You'd best forget all about this, Layla. It will only make your every day sour with regret."

"I'll have as much regret as it takes," Layla whispered. "I'll have all the regret in the world, but I'll never, ever for-get this. I'd rather have all the sourness in the world, you nasty bird. I'd rather weep my heart out every night than go on freezing inside. Go, go away with all your mean words of caution. I'll never, ever listen to them again."

And for one last time, for one last chime, that seven-charmed bracelet rang out in the castle.

Ding!

Which left Layla all alone, next to her slumbering Prince.

With all caution gone to the winds.

With a heart full of love, that gazed at his sweet, sleeping face.

With no recollection at all of any rule.

14
the weavers
and spinners

Oh, how the Winds started to storm.

The whole castle shook with their anger. Never had she heard the Winds so furious. She could hear crystals shattering, she could see the velvet and satin flapping, she could feel the whole edifice of her dreams cracking, falling apart, rent by the Winds' speechless fury.

She had broken the Rule.

She would have to pay.

She would be made to pay.

Dearly.

Oh, how they shrieked at her.

Layla's whole body was shaking, her hair flying about her face as wild as panic. She knew, she knew what it was the Winds wanted to say.

In spite of herself she found her reflection in the window and glanced at her frantic eyes, looking for some shred of hope, of mercy even, telling herself she wasn't to blame for all of this, none of it really—not the Prince, not the scooter, not even those long years of listening to the Winds' wily counsel. She couldn't be blamed for that careless bridal shrug, years and years back, that had made them all fall asleep to the Loveless Lullaby.

Yet . . .

She had made that vow. She had promised to remember her sister, always. What would happen now? What would these Winds ask for now? Who would be made to pay?

Layla couldn't help but look. She couldn't help delving deep into her eyes, trying to find what it was that had made her risk so much.

Wondering if it was really worth it.

And the horrid words slowly came to her lips.

"You fool, you selfish, stupid fool, no one there in your thoughts but your own silly heart. No thought for anyone, huh Layla? Look at you now, look at you, look at your wild eyes, you madwoman. You're all alone now, this Wind will never stop blowing. Luna will never come back now. You've finally killed your own sister, Layla, and as for the living ones, they'll never, ever speak to you again. You might as well stay here Layla , there really isn't anything to go back to anymore.

"You'll have nothing now," shrieked the Winds. "We'll make sure of that. Forget your house, your sisters. Forget your girls, we'll blow about you every day of your miserable life, Layla. We'll blow so hard you won't be hearing anything else at all, and you'll know, you'll know Layla, this was all your fault. Because you wouldn't stop in time. Because you were too greedy. So utterly, selfishly greedy.

"It doesn't take more than a moment, Layla, one moment of forgetting everything but your own foolish heart. One moment like that is enough to show what you're really made of, Layla. You would give it all away, you would sell everyone down the river for one silly, sleeping Prince. Who, mind you, hasn't even woken up yet. Who hasn't done a single thing for you yet. Who hasn't had to pay any price at all. It isn't his sisters, it isn't his girls, oh no, it's all your very own price to pay, Layla, and you have no one to blame but yourself!"

Oh, she was sobbing, as wild as a madwoman, as wild as a desert storm. "Take Luna," she shrieked. "Take her, she's been yours since the day she was born, just like the rest of us. Take the Prince, take this castle, take everything, just let me keep my girls!"

"Why should you keep anything?" the Winds' mocking voice replied. "Why should we let you have anything at all? You, who have betrayed so much, who suddenly gives up on her dear little sister, as easy as casting off a painful old shoe."

"Oh, you've played Luna for all she was worth," Layla said, calmer now that her sobs had dried her all out. "You can have her. I've paid enough for her visits. I've paid enough for those tea parties. Take her, she has been yours forever anyway. Take all of them, but why did all the rest of it have to be so cruel? Why couldn't you let me stay here? Why, why couldn't I have my daughters too? Why did it all have to be so cruel?"

"It doesn't really have to be, Layla," said the elf, who suddenly showed up right there, near her bed, peaceful as always, as if this storm never even touched him, bringing his own little island of quiet, which no Wind could touch. "It doesn't really have to be so cruel," repeated the elf. "It's your choice to make, you know."

"How can you say that," she retorted, swift with fury. "All this talk about choices. I haven't any, don't you see? You sound like Liora, you, who promised so much, you, who gave me so much that I actually started to want more. You, who told me I could stop listening to the Winds, you said it would be all right."

"And it will," said the elf, ever so patiently. "It really will be all right, Layla. Because you see, even though Liora makes as perfect sense as ever, she doesn't know about me. She knows all about rules. She knows all about give and take. But she never had me for a friend. She never had someone just sitting there in her corner waiting for her every wish. And as far as I can tell, that was a wish I heard just now, as desperate a wish as anyone could ever hope to earn."

"Why, why are you sitting there waiting for my every wish?" Layla asked weepily. "Won't you tell me once and for all?"

"Remember, Layla, I told you long ago, you are our heroine."

"And I asked you who's 'we.'"

"We? We are the wish-granters," replied the elf, standing taller than ever. "We are the makers of dreams, the weavers of longing, the spinners of yarn. But that's not to say we haven't any wishes of our own. You see, Layla, we do have our wishes, we have our little agenda here, perhaps a bet or two with those who never really wished you well.

"And so we, we the wish-granters, we wish to grant you this: that you shall indeed have it all, the cake and the stick and the omelet, whatever. To eat and to have, to have and to hold, to love and to cherish. All of it, Layla. The Prince, the castle, the girls. Any one of your sisters who would like to be charmed by a wish. Anything, Layla. Each and every wish you would care to make."

"How come?" she asked yet again, her eyes as wide as the day she was born.

"Why me?" she chirped, just a bit hoarse with amazement.

"Because," said the elf. "Because you've wished so hard. Because you truly believed it to be your last wish ever. And because we would like—just for once, just to make us happy—to have a story turn out really well.

"And it will be your story, Layla. You of all women, among all the broken-hearted, among all the disillusioned and sober, the sad and the bitter, you, you Layla, shall have a tale with a happy end."

And she did.

Yes, dearest, just like that.

acknowledgments

Writing this book was a long and difficult journey, and many thanks are due. First of all, to my friend and reader, Michal Shechter, who knows how to put her finger on just the right places. Also to Haim Rechnitzer, for a fabulous, day-long conversation about evil winds and their tricks. Thanks to Gai Ad, Eva Jablonka, Adi Arbel, and Merav Shaul for early readings, and to Amit Rotbard for her timely help and encouragement. A huge, special thank-you to my gentle agent, Chandler Crawford, and to Ziv Lewis, who helped me find her. Thanks to my editor, Tracy Carns, for believing that magic still works. Mostly, thanks to Daniel Dor—my sweet, lovely Danny—who said it was time to grow, and was there with me every step of the way.